To Richard and Phoebe, with all my love.

TABLE OF CONTENTS

ENGLAND

ONE

The dog had the street to himself. He paused to sniff the corner of a cottage then lifted his leg and marked his territory before he padded on down the dozing street and disappeared around the corner. Nothing else moved. A quiet Sunday in summer, only the occasional drone of a bee to break the silence. The sun reflected off cottages unchanged in three hundred years – front doors opening directly onto the narrow street. Small homes touching shoulders, lining both sides of the street, crowded around the church. A door opened – the sound of organ music followed by first one voice then many. Footsteps clattered on the cobbled pathway from the church and out through the passageway of the gatehouse onto the street. Matins was over. The congregation dispersed to their cars or to the pub opposite for a noontime drink before returning home for Sunday dinner. The street settled back again, basking in the sun.

A car came slowly down the deserted street as if its driver was looking for an address, unfamiliar with the surroundings. It paused briefly at the 15th century gatehouse then rounded the corner and parked just off the road by the millstream. A man got out and came back to where the car had paused, hugging the thick stone walls of the churchyard as he rounded the corner.

He stopped in the empty street and scanned the gatehouse, the original medieval entrance to the church property. A passage with thick stone walls and cobbled floor cut right through the old building. Next to the entrance on the street side, covered stone steps led up to the room above the passageway. Within the passage itself, a thick oak door on the right hand wall led to a small museum – two rooms of local artifacts – church records dating back to 1354; maps of the original parish showing the three communal "Great Fields" where crops were rotated each year on the strips of land allocated to every villager; local events; old pictures; old photographs – everything that had gone into making the village what it was today. He tried the centuries-old door. The museum was closed. He stepped back into the shadows of the opposite wall and looked at the door carefully, taking in the massive old frame and the huge iron hinges. Then he casually ambled on into the churchyard, his eyes adjusting to the bright sunlight as he came out of the passageway.

He looked around, craning his neck to look up at the crooked spire with the weathervane on top, and at the surrounding hills dotted with sheep and wind-blown trees leaning away from the frequent south-westerly gales blowing in from the Atlantic. For ten minutes he wandered through the churchyard stopping to read the centuries old gravestones. No one was around, it was a peaceful sunny afternoon. He felt in a time warp.

Presently he returned to the museum as if waiting for someone. The museum was still closed but he tried the massive old oak door once again, just to make sure. He looked around, saw no one, and turned his attention to the door frame, then reached into his jacket pocket and pulled out a folded paper which he unwrapped. Inside were five toothpicks, each coded with a different colored top. He selected the blue one, and held it between his teeth while he carefully refolded the paper with the remaining four and replaced them in his pocket. He turned again to the door frame and this time he reached up with his left hand and fingered the overhead lintel, searching with his fingers until he found a centuries' old split in the beam, invisible from the ground. With his left hand marking the spot, he took the toothpick from between his teeth and with his right hand carefully pushed it into the crack until only the blue top showed above the wood. He stepped back from the door to confirm that it would not be noticed by a casual observer, and satisfied he walked back into the sunny churchyard and wandered passed the church, down a driveway lined with ancient beech trees and left through a different gate to return to his car.

He looked at his watch – 1:30 on a lazy summer afternoon and he had accomplished what he had come to do. No trouble, no observers, but no explanations. He wished he knew what he had done – and why, but those had been the rules. It had paid for the rental car and a weekend of expenses, and here he was on the beautiful North Atlantic coast, on a perfect summer day with the beach less than three miles away. He backed out onto the street and at the crossroads gunned his car across the main road and up the hill on his way to the shore. Five minutes later with the ocean glistening in the distance, the car dropped down through the winding narrow lanes onto the main coast road and he was heading to the sea.

She was waiting for him at the head of the carpark. She waved and came towards the car, barefoot and treading gingerly on the rough gravel. "Did you do it?"

He nodded, unexpectedly finding himself embarrassed and a little guilty. "Which one?"

"The blue."

"Why blue?"

"I waited ten minutes and there was no one around, there were no cars in the carpark and the weather was fine, so I used the blue."

"Did anyone see you?"

"No. Enough about that." "Don't forget you're not supposed to know anything, give it a rest."

She looked at him closely, "What's wrong?"

"I damn well hope it's as innocent as it seems," he said as he got his beach gear out of the car, "It just makes me uneasy. It's pretty weird when you think about it."

"Well at least the weather's gorgeous, so let's enjoy it," she said in a quieter tone, sobered by his second thoughts.

It had been three months earlier, again on a Sunday, their whole lives seemed to be made up of Sundays, their only schedule-free day of the week – a lazy morning having a relaxed breakfast in the local diner, when she had looked up from perusing a newspaper that a previous customer had left on their table.,

"You'll be in the UK in July, won't you?"

He answered that he would be and asked why she wanted to know.

She had laughed and passed the paper over to him and he had read the personal ad she pointed to.

"You're always talking about wanting to get back to Devon, maybe this is your chance!"

They both laughed – but later that

> Are you planning to be in England this July? Do me a favor and I'll pay for a weekend on the Atlantic Coast. Write Box 55.

day after she had left to return to her work in Philadelphia he had picked up the paper again and on impulse had torn out the ad, stuck a Post-it on it with only his mobile number and the dates when he would be in the UK, stuffed it in an envelope and the next day on his way to work had thrown it in the mail. It was something they could joke about the following weekend when he went to Philadelphia.

They had been together for almost two years and had developed a routine that worked for both of them, one weekend in New York, the next in Philly, they were close, comfortable with the current set up, both working at their careers and valuing their independence.

But he didn't mention it the following weekend because by then he had got a call. A very pleasant voice thanked him enthusiastically for answering the ad, and explained that it was a very small thing that was needed – completely innocent, "No drugs or bombs or anything like that." The caller went on to add that for several reasons it was impossible for him to be there himself – which was why he needed help from someone who would be in England in July. He had gone on to apologize for being unable to give any further information, but stressed it was not dangerous – all expenses would be paid and the only thing that he must agree to was absolute secrecy, he could tell no one.

After the call had ended he had checked the log on his mobile and had found the call was marked "Unavailable." He had attempted to call back anyway but had got nowhere, just an empty line. He had kicked himself for getting involved so fast and could not believe that he had actually agreed to help. The voice on the phone had said he would be receiving further instructions so he had decided to wait and see how he felt when he knew more, figuring he could always back out if he didn't like what developed. It had all sounded very strange, but he was going to be in England anyway, and an extra, all expenses paid weekend in Devon, had been appealing, and besides, why not help the man out – it was no skin off his back.... He remembered the area fondly from family vacations there when he was growing up, when the company his father worked for had assigned him to their UK office.

The following week the "voice" texted him telling him to take five flat toothpicks and paint the tips of each one with a different color, one blue, one yellow, one green, one orange and one red. The text had apologized for the inconvenience, and noted that without his address painted ones could not be mailed to him. In a way that had been reassuring – obviously the voice was not that sophisticated with technology where a quick search would probably have revealed his whole life, it had been good to think that he was as anonymous to the voice, as the voice was to him. He had tried to reply to the message with no success, had saved the number of the text and had done a quick Google search for more information, but had had no success, which he had found frustrating and slightly unsettling...

Over the following weeks there had been several more texts – snippets of additional information, none of which seemed to be complete. Not all of them from the same number and as with the first one he had replied to them but got no further response. He had saved the numbers, and tried to trace their source but had always come up against a brick wall, which worried him. But by then he realized he was hooked....

By June he had most of the information he needed – the area in Devon he was to go to; the place he had to find when he got there, and what to do with the toothpicks.

It had been getting more and more difficult not to tell her about it – and more and more he had wondered what he had committed himself to. For her part, more and more she had been wondering what was wrong, aware of his increasing tension. So it was she who had finally broached the subject the next time they were together. It was the opening he had needed to let her in to what had been going on for the past three months.

Her first reaction had been laughter, "You really answered that ad?" Sheepishly he said, "Yes, I thought we would get a laugh out of it."

"So what's the problem?" She said, "I'm laughing."

He had gone on to explain his rising doubts each time he had received another text, and his increasing concern when he hadn't been able to trace the source of any of them.

"Did you think to save the numbers and everything?"

"Of course I did, I'm not that big a fool!"

"The whole thing had seemed pretty harmless," he added, but he had been getting increasingly concerned about the request for secrecy and the anonymity of the texts.

She tried to reassure him. "I'm sure it's harmless, it's probably someone with too much money who has a bet with a friend that he can't plant the toothpick without being seen – or it could be one of those international scavenger hunts that are set up on social media, they would need total secrecy."

It worked, he felt much better – he felt a fool to have worried.

"Tell you what." She said. "If you do it the weekend before your meetings, I can come over with you and we'll have a romantic couple of days in Devon and you can drive me back to the airport on Monday morning."

He thought for a second. "That would work – my first meeting is not until Tuesday – but I don't want you to come with me when I do it, I don't want you involved."

"Fine with me." She replied. "If the sun's shining, drop me at the beach first, and if it'd raining park me in a pub – I'll soak up some local atmosphere while you're doing the deed!"

So it had been agreed, they would both fly out on Friday evening from New York, she would fly back to Philadelphia on the following Monday afternoon and he would stay on for his meetings.

TWO

A month later they had arrived at Heathrow very early on a Saturday morning – mist still rising from the ground – and had taken the shuttle to pick up their rental car. Within the hour they were booked into the hotel in central London where his company had made reservations for the following week. A quick breakfast and they hit the road for Devon, planning to find a bed and breakfast to stay that night and Sunday. What they hadn't planned for was the mass of holiday makers making their way to the beaches of the Southwest to take advantage of the great weekend weather forecast. Four hours later they were still on the A303 looking down at Stonehenge.

He nudged her. "Hey, you want to see Stonehenge? Well, there it is." Half an hour passed and they were still stuck on the road, watching the crowds circling the metal fencing that kept them well away from the monument.

"When I was a kid living here you could walk right up and touch the stones and walk in and out of them. It was much better without the barriers – but I guess they are trying to preserve it."

He went silent, remembering his first visit with his mother and father. It felt a long time ago. Events he had locked away from himself and everyone else came flooding back. He had been hiding behind one of the stones, waiting to jump out at his parents when they passed – and then he heard his mother and father arguing – his father's voice low and intense, his mother's rising and falling, passionate, doing most of the talking, his father occasionally answering in monosyllables. It had been the end of his happy life, taking for granted the close family unit his mother and father had provided. It had never occurred to him that it could change – trust was a given, but after that he did not know the meaning of the word. He had never again relied on others to make his decisions, it was the beginning of his life on his own.

"This place brings back a lot of memories." He said, almost under his breath, almost to himself.

"Good memories?" She asked.

"'I'll tell you sometime…."

The traffic edged forward and he looked in the side mirror before changing lanes hoping a different lane would move faster.

Finally, they were clear of traffic jams and heading for the coast again, but soon they both decided they were ready to take a break and started to look for somewhere to stay that night. It meant that they would still be about an hour way from their destination, but the added hours on the road, and all the traffic jams had taken their toll – and jet lag was kicking in.

They turned off onto a country road pointing towards Exmoor, and wound their way through several small market towns until finally they reached the edge of the moors. They found themselves on a twisting road, steep wooded hills coming right down to the edge of the road on one side then levelling off to low lying fields and a meandering stream on the other. A few miles further on they saw a picturesque pub tucked up under the hill – its sign boasting its Stagecoach Inn pedigree, and parked the car. Outside were the ubiquitous tables and umbrellas common to all pubs, but inside, the inn remained genuinely old with low beamed ceilings and stone floors. They ordered a light lunch to eat outside, and took their drinks back out into the sun to wait. They were both exhausted and when they found that the inn had a vacancy they booked the room for both that night and for Sunday and after lunch climbed the stairs to their room and collapsed on the bed for an early afternoon nap, too tired to even joke about the four poster bed they found there….

They were woken several hours later by the sun low in the sky shining into their window. They turned to each other and made slow unhurried love. Finally, it was sinking in that they were on vacation and they basked in the luxury of no schedules. They had all the time in the world. Sometime later they got ready for dinner and went down to the bar for drinks. When they told the bartender they were heading for the coast in the morning, he warned them to get on the road early ahead of the weekend traffic from London. So after their meal in the adjacent dining room, and one after-dinner drink back in the bar, they said their goodnights to the friendly group there and went back upstairs to their room.

They took the bartender's advice and were up early Sunday morning. A quick breakfast, then back in their car to complete the rest of their journey. It was another beautiful day and they were anxious to get the one thing he had to do out of the way so they could spend as much time as possible on the beach.

They drove in silence for much of the way, he now focusing on his immediate task, she suddenly finding herself worrying about his safety, suddenly it did not seem like a lark anymore. *Why had she pointed out that damn ad to him and why had he answered it? They didn't need the money, they could easily have come to Devon by themselves – they just hadn't thought to do it. Why hadn't they?* It made her think about their crushing schedules, the last twenty-four-hours had left her wondering if they were forgetting how to relax and enjoy themselves – and each other.

He broke into her thoughts. "I'm going to go straight to the beach and drop you off so we can get this over with."

They drove on through the village that he would be returning to after he had left her, and two miles later turned the car down the steep access road to the ocean. He told the carpark attendant that he was dropping off his friend, then turned to her, put his arm around her shoulders, and kissed her.

"Give me an about an hour and I'll be back."

"I'll meet you here in the car park a bit before two." She replied, trying to sound as if she hadn't a care in the world. Then added, "Good luck, and please be careful."

He promised he would be, then circled the parking kiosk and disappeared up the hill and onto the road back to the village.

She watched his car until it rounded the curve out of sight then turned and walked across the carpark and down the sandy path between the dunes out onto the beach.

In front of her stretched miles and miles of sand and far beyond the sea, and from where she stood she could hear the hypnotic sound of the waves. She passed the hut renting surfboards, and glanced at a sign posting the times of high and low tide. The tide was at its low ebb and about to turn. A group of people in wet suits were milling around outside the hut anxiously scanning the ocean, waiting for the large Atlantic breakers to get bigger and stronger as the sea began its steady advance up the beach.

She kept her sandals on until she was through the high tide flotsam then barefoot started the long walk towards the sea. Five minutes later she reached the edge of the waves and started walking along in the shallows, water rippling over her feet. A warm salty breeze and the sound of the waves mesmerized her and she felt herself let go and relax. She turned and looked back the way she had come, really taking in her surroundings for the first time. The beauty of the view took her breath away. To her left, rocks and then a cliff framed the beach. Diagonal steps cut into the cliff led to a large white hotel sitting imposingly above, but to her right vast stretches of sands disappeared far into the distance. She could just make out where the sand dunes ended at an inlet, and just make out faint blue and purple hills on the far side.

Time slipped away and suddenly she realized she had been walking for some time and needed to start back to the carpark.

She got there just in time. Delightedly she saw his car coming down the hill. She waved and came towards the car, barefoot and treading gingerly on the rough gravel.

"Did you do it?"

He nodded. A few more questions from her and he cut her off.

"Enough about that, give it a rest." Belatedly he felt a fool to have got involved.... He hoped that it was all as innocent as he had been told. He had allowed himself to be used and did not like the feeling.

She looked at him closely, sensing his tension.

"Well at least the weather's gorgeous, so let's enjoy it," she said in a quieter tone.

He got his gear out of the car and they went down to the beach.

They walked on the wet sand parallel to the sea for a long time, and after ten minutes she could tell he was starting to relax, the rhythmic sound of the waves starting to work their magic. The tide was coming in fast, chasing them further and further out of the shallows with each advancing wave. The Wet Suit Brigade paddled their boards out beyond the waves, waiting for the perfect ride.

They stood together hand in hand and watched the swells forming again and again way out in the ocean, growing in size as they rolled in, curling up higher and higher and then cresting fifty yards out, crashing down with a loud roar and rolling in until they finally petered out in the shallows. They watched for a long time before turning back towards the car.

As they walked back they could see waiters serving people on the patio of the big white hotel on the cliff-top and decided to take a break before heading back to the inn. Half an hour later they were seated on the patio with the other customers enjoying cool drinks and appetizers.

He breathed out heavily. "God, this is so great, it takes me back to when I was here as a kid."

He paused, as a new thought came to him – he turned to her.

"I have a lot of vacation due, how about you? Could you come back the week after next? My meetings finish up on Friday and we could stay the following week and really have time to be together."

Regretfully she replied that she couldn't make it that week – she had a heavy work schedule that she couldn't shift around, it was a shame because the week after that she would have come like a shot.

It suddenly occurred to him that he needed to let go and stop limiting the depth of their relationship. For the first time that he could remember he felt open to risk being vulnerable – it was a new thought and an exciting one...

"OK." He said. "I'll take two weeks, you come over for the second week and in between I'll re-discover my childhood haunts, I've always wanted to do that. Will you come, please?"

She laughed out loud. "That sounds really great, yes, of course I'll come, what a great idea, but I can't believe you're actually going to stay away from work for two whole weeks!"

"It's time." He answered. "Besides, we both need a break and to be together for more than thirty-six hours at a time."

They finished their drinks and on an impulse on the way out he stopped at the front desk and made a reservation for both weeks.

"Done! Decided and booked!" He said, "But there's one more thing I'd like to do before we head back to the inn – "

"No!" she broke in.

You don't know what I was going to say." He protested.

"Yes I do – you want to go back and see if that damn toothpick is still there! Let it go, it's over. Besides, it's going to take us at least two hours to get back to the inn and I'm getting hungry for dinner already."

He acquiesced but made a mental note to check it out the following weekend after his meetings were over.

But he didn't let it go – once they were in the car he brought it up again. "Come on," he said. "It will only take a minute, we practically go past the church on the way back."

Reluctantly she agreed – besides, he was driving so she figured she didn't have many options, she knew how determined he was when he got an idea in his head.

"OK, but I don't think it's a good idea." She said.

Soon they were back at the church and parked in the carpark attached to the pub. They crossed the road to the gatehouse and the entrance to the museum. Casually he ran his fingers along the top of the lintel.

"It's gone."

Somehow it was not what either of them had expected.

"Wow!" she said.

He insisted that they walk on into the churchyard in case someone had been watching them and they toured the old grave stones for a while before returning to the pub carpark.

"I need a drink." He said.

They went into the pub and joined the crowd already there. She sat down at a table while he fetched them beers from the bar. He came back with the drinks looking tense.

"What's up?" She asked.

"See that man leaning on the bar talking to the bartender?"

She looked towards the bar.

"Don't let him see you looking!"

He sat down, his back to the bar.

"He's one of those friendly types – too friendly, like he's looking for someone. He asked if we were on holiday. I told him we had been on the beach for the day and were heading back to London, and just in case he'd seen us going into the church yard I told him we were both history buffs."

"Now you're being paranoid." She broke in.

I don't think so," he answered. "Did I tell you he was picking his teeth with a toothpick? And that the toothpick had a painted blue top?"

They finished their beers slowly so not to draw attention then got up and made for the door.

The bartender called out, "Goodnight, come again."

They both turned and waved.

"Cheers!" He called back as they made their exit.

The drive back to the inn was uneventful – and silent – although they both found themselves surreptitiously looking back to make sure they weren't being followed. It was a relief when they finally reached the inn.

"No headlights following us!" He joked as they got out of the car.

But it wasn't until they were in the dining room eating the local trout and drinking a glass of wine that they both felt back to normal.

"Not quite the weekend I envisioned." she said softly, "Do you think we're being paranoid?"

This time it was he who comforted her.

"It's probably that we're in an unfamiliar place, you lose your judgement about what is normal. I think we probably over reacted. Let's put it behind us, I'm so glad we planned our vacation and that you'll be back in two weeks. By the time we finally fly back to the States after that we won't even remember any of this."

On the way up to their room his phone vibrated – a new message had arrived. He read it, not recognizing the sender and his stomach turned over.

"Who's it from? Is it bad news?" she had seen his reaction.

"It's from the ad guy, just wanting to thank me for placing the toothpick." He replied.

But that wasn't all the message had said. It requested that he place two more toothpicks.

They took their time in the morning. Her plane was not until 4:00pm so they had a lazy breakfast before heading back to Heathrow Airport. After their experience getting down to Devon, they decided to take the northern route, sticking to the motorways all the way back to London. They headed out on the M5 and outside Bristol merged onto the M4 for the rest of the journey. Traffic was still heavy but at least they did not come to a complete stop as they had on the way down.

As he drove he was thinking about the text .... *Should he tell her?... She would be against him getting even more involved... He did not want her to go back to the States worrying – or with them arguing. He knew she would think him crazy.*

Finally, he took his phone out of his pocket and tossed it into her lap.

"Read the text I got last night."

She read it in silence. "Jesus! You're not going to do it, are you?"

"Hell, I'm involved up to my neck already – I'm not sure I have an option. He obviously knows who I am and where we are."

"Don't do it! Just ignore it." She said, knowing in advance he would not change his mind.

She read the text again, looking for ammunition.

"And what's this bit about – *add the orange or red toothpicks for caution or danger if anyone sees you*? What the hell are you getting into? This is not a joke anymore, please don't get any more involved! What will they want you to do next? I'm really worried about this. Just stop now.... Please!"

"I promise I'll be careful and I will go to the police if I get worried – maybe even before I do what he is asking.... and just maybe I'll find out what this is all about."

She exploded. "You're crazy!"

They drove in silence for a while.

She tried again. "You could just block his texts, or just not answer them."

"Of course I could," he said sarcastically. "That would solve everything." He watched as she forwarded the text message to her phone.

"What are you going to do with that?"

"I'm going to try and track it down while I'm back home, where are the other messages, can you forward them to me?"

"They're back in the apartment – for some reason I deleted them from my phone."

She swallowed hard, trying to stay silent, she didn't want to start quarreling when she was about to get on the plane. She was worried what would happen next, who knew what else he would be asked to do? *What kind of a quagmire was he getting into?* ... She was determined to find out what was going on once she was back in the States.

A little time later she changed the subject, "What happened when you went to Stonehenge as a kid? You said you would tell me."

"I heard my father telling my mother that he had fallen for a woman at work. I was hiding behind one of the stones waiting to jump out and surprise them and they did not realize I could hear them."

"How awful for you."

"Yeah, it was." He accelerated to pass a large articulated truck, "I jumped out and confronted them, yelling and screaming, I was pretty dramatic – it's probably why they built the fence around the Monument."

"Don't joke about it! It must have been terrible."

"Yeah, it was." He repeated, quietly this time.

She asked what had happened and he reverted to his laconic style, "They got a divorce. Mom and I went back to the States and he stayed in England shacking up with his woman friend."

"Did you stay in touch?"

"No it was a messy, ugly divorce and I have no idea what happened to him, he might be in the car ahead for all I know I wouldn't recognize him – or he could be long dead. He's always been dead to me; it makes no difference."

"What about your Mother?"

21

"Now there was one bitter lady, angry to her dying day."

He turned and looked at her, "Can we please change the subject? – This conversation in this traffic and there will be a road rage incident if another truck cuts me off."

They were not going to return the rental car – he had several meetings in locations outside London, and around two o'clock they arrived at the drop-off in front of Terminal 4. He got out of the car and got her case out of the trunk.

He looked at her tenderly.

"I can't wait for you to come back, two weeks is an awful long time, but we'll have a lot of time to talk then."

They stood with their arms around each other.

She couldn't stop herself, "Why didn't you tell me about your parents before? – You told me they were dead."

"I don't know – I hid it all from myself as well as you. I guess it was my way of surviving."

"Thank you for telling me." She said soberly. "Maybe I'll share some of my secrets when I get back."

"That would be nice!" He answered, trying to lighten what had become a serious conversation.

"I wish you would forget about placing more damn toothpicks though, that really worries me." She pleaded, "Please don't do it!"

He kissed her, "I promise I'll be careful. And I will go to the authorities if I don't like the smell of it."

"No one will believe you," She answered.

They kissed goodbye again, both looking forward to her return in a couple of weeks.

He watched her walk into the terminal and up to the counter.

She turned, saw that he was still there watching her, blew him a kiss and waved before disappearing down the escalator to go through security.

THREE

The following week was uneventful. After he had dropped her off, he had gone back to his hotel and prepared for his meetings the next day. They texted frequently and within twenty-four hours she had let him know her travel arrangements for the second week of the vacation – they agreed that she would take the train down to Devon and he would be at the station to meet her. He reminded her to check the weekend train schedule, since she would be arriving on Saturday, and she told him that she would text him when she was actually on the train to let him know what time she got in.

The meetings went well with no surprises but he found time dragging. He was missing her more than usual and his head was already focused on their vacation, still almost a week away. So he was delighted when he found Friday's meeting had been cancelled. And even better news, Thursday's meeting was in Plymouth so he would already be in Devon. *Great*, he thought, *I'll get started on my vacation a day early!* He began to look forward to the drive across the moors to the North Devon coast on Friday. He called the hotel to see if he could bring his arrival date forward by one day and was told that it would not be a problem. Then he texted her to let her know of his change of plans, telling her he was counting the days until they were back together.

Friday morning, he was up early. He didn't care for Plymouth that much – its romantic history of seafaring explorers and naval warfare fell flat for him and he found the city to be crowded and uninteresting. He realized he much preferred Devon's north Atlantic coast with its history of smugglers and wreckers, to the south coast which faced the English Channel. He found south Devon crowded and tamed, but both coasts, he realized, were now much more developed than when he had lived in England as a boy.

He headed out of Plymouth driving north on the Tavistock Road – and stopped in Tavistock briefly for coffee. Apart from Starbucks the town seemed to him to be stuck in a Victorian time warp, a small country town built into the hills on the edge of Dartmoor, everyone taking their time as if they were on a perpetual vacation. Refreshed he continued on, through Peter Tavy and Mary Tavy – wondering what had been the dynamics between the siblings that they both had to have their own villages... He was fascinated by the Devon names – Sheepwash; Lady Cross; Folly Gate; Fairy Cross; Winkleigh Barton ...

With time no object, he purposely took back roads across Dartmoor and then Exmoor, his car rumbling over the road grids designed to keep the wild ponies in protected areas, stopping when he felt like it. Mid-afternoon he arrived in Blackmoor Gate and followed the signs to the coast road through Combe Martin, to Ilfracombe then up to Mullacott Cross.

On the coast road north of his final destination, he came to where he was to place the second toothpick and found another Victorian Era town – with a couple of incongruous nods to the present in a theater complex looking remarkably like the twin cooling towers of a nuclear reactor, and a huge bronze statue of a woman overlooking the harbor, sword raised in one hand and guts prominently displayed – *placed there to scare those entering the harbor,* he figured.

He climbed the steep path on the hill above the harbor to a small thirteenth century chapel – from the eighteenth century on it had also doubled as a lighthouse, keeping ships off the famously rocky North Devon coast. He walked into the cramped interior space, seeing first the chapel –the altar placed in front of the window facing out to sea, keeping watch. The second room was now a museum but still had the huge original open fireplace from when the rooms housed the lighthouse keeper and his family. And it was there he was to place the toothpick. He waited until a man and a woman left, made sure that no more visitors were about to reach the chapel, then felt in his pocket and pulled out the same folded paper with the remaining four toothpicks. He was suddenly hesitant... *Christ! Should I be doing this? ... How stupid is this.... Why didn't I throw these damn things away after the first one...? if I'd thought about it, I should have realized that there was a reason for five toothpicks.... I should just walk back down the hill now and chuck them in the nearest trash bin... Why am I so damn rigid that I always have to finish what I've started?....* Normally he took pride in this trait of his character, but this time he wasn't so sure...

He went ahead anyway and stuck the toothpick with the yellow tip in a mortar crack at the back of the narrow stone mantel as the text had requested.

He left quickly, down the steep path to where he had left his car, hoping no one had seen him. It had been a long drive, made longer by his meandering route over the moors, and he would be glad when he reached the hotel.

Seven miles further, and he came to the village and to the gatehouse entrance of the 14th century church, where he had stuck the first toothpick in the frame of the door in the passageway into the churchyard, and on a whim stopped in at the old pub opposite the church for a quick beer – ignoring her voice in his head telling him to *let it go!* It was a busy Friday evening, but the man with the toothpick was nowhere to be seen. He finished his beer and left, finally reaching the hotel early in the evening

FOUR

Saturday morning, he woke to the sound of rain beating against the windows. His room faced the ocean and he saw a rough sea with huge waves, much bigger than the previous week, roaring into the beach. The surfboard contingent was already out even at that early hour. He dressed and went down to breakfast and was told by his optimistic waiter, that the rain would stop and it would be fine later. Remembering the Devon weather, he resisted asking him to define the word *"fine"*.

But the rain did stop by midday, although the sun did not come out, and he took off for a run along the three mile stretch of sand to the mouth of the estuary where two rivers joined and flowed into the sea. He vaguely remembered from his childhood being told about a lighthouse at the mouth of the estuary but when he had talked to his waiter at breakfast he had been told that the old lighthouse had been destroyed by storms in the 1950's and had been replaced by an automatic light mounted on metal stilts.

"Not so picturesque," the waiter said, "But it does the job. Don't go much further into the Burrows." He added, "There's a restricted area that you have to keep out of, it's used by the Military, for training or something. You'll see the, "Keep Out" signs and electrified fencing – and if a red flag is flying it's a warning that they're using live ammunition, keep clear!" ..... "Besides," the waiter added as an afterthought as he cleared the table, "They never found all the land mines that were planted in the dunes in World War Two. Treading on one of those could spoil your day..."

He wasn't sure if his waiter was giving him good advice or just had a morose sense of humor, but he thanked him for the information, and told him he would heed his warnings.

He ran until he reached the estuary. It was wider than he had thought and through the mist, on the far side, he could just make out several miniature villages. On his side, a couple of fishing boats were beached waiting for the tide to come in and closer to the dunes were the skeletons of several wrecks. Below the high tide mark the sand changed to pebbles and then dark indigo mud sloping down to the channel winding inland filled with startling blue water. He looked around, deciding whether to climb up into the sand dunes or leave that for another day. He could see two people in the distance lying on top of one of the dunes looking through binoculars. Bird watchers he thought. He decided not to disturb them and turned and ran back along the wet sand below the high tide mark towards the hotel.

As he ran, his thoughts returned to last Sunday night at the Inn when they were going up to bed after their day at the coast. The text had been an unwelcome surprise. The request to place two additional toothpicks before the next Sunday had given him pause for thought, but after he had made the decision to do it, he knew he would complete the task exactly as the text had requested. The Sunday deadline had been a whole week away and he had figured that he had plenty of time. Now he realized that he had not allowed for his work schedule and travel taking up most of the week. Today was Saturday. Tomorrow was Sunday. *One more and it was done...* He should do it today. *Let's get this thing over with...* Still plenty of time for a quick trip, and where he had to go was only about eight miles southeast of his hotel.

So after lunch he got in his car and took the main road inland back through the village where he had placed the first toothpick and on to the old market town built on one of the two rivers. He wondered what was the significance of the locations where he had put the toothpicks, or if the real significance was the area within the triangle formed by the locations. He reminded himself to look carefully at a map when he got back to the hotel to see if he could figure out why he had been directed to those specific places.

Once in the town it took time to negotiate the obtuse traffic patterns, but finally he arrived in the center, on a street parallel to the "pedestrianized" *(A term he had learnt from his guide book)* High Street, and managed to find space in a two-story parking garage on a side-street off the main thoroughfare. Across from him was the historic center of the old town. A cobblestone walk-way cut through the middle, and he could just see tall wrought-iron gates opening onto a street at the other end. The walk-way was bordered on one side by a massive stone wall that enclosed a cemetery and an ancient granite building. The other side was more open, with eighteen century buildings and a few pockets of manicured grass. The serenity of the area was broken only by the clatter of the pedestrians cutting through to shop in the High Street at the far end.

He was beginning to wonder if the guy he had agreed to help was some kind of history buff with definite religious nut overtones – all three of the buildings, including the one he was about to go to, belonged to a church – and all were old, dating from the thirteenth and fourteenth centuries. This time he was looking for a fourteenth century chapel and chantry.

It was hard to miss. Next door to an old church with an impressive spire, the two buildings dominated the remnants of the historic part of the town. He had read in the guide book that a tower had been added to the chantry by the Tudors, and the Victorians had added steps up to the entrance in the tower and were the architects of the massive stone wall that bordered the walk-way and surrounded the cemetery – including the chantry standing out there alone in the middle of the graves.

He pondered the best way to reach the old building.... He ignored the Tudor tower, realizing immediately that going up the steps to the door in the tower would more than likely lead to a dead end, he would never be able to find his way down to get out into the cemetery, even if one existed.... And there was no way he could jump over the wall without being seen either, this was Saturday afternoon and the cobblestone cut-through was busy. The obvious way was to go in through the cemetery,

28

and he hoped that once he was in, it would be easy to get around to the far side of the chantry and to the entrance to the crypt.

He followed the stone wall back the way he had come until it turned the corner and continued down another small lane. On one side was the entrance to the old parish church, and on the other, a short way further on, he found iron gates set into the stone wall. The gates were not locked. He opened one of them and walked through – finally he was inside the cemetery wall!

He started across the old burial grounds to the chantry – the grass still wet from the recent rain squelched under his feet with every step. He trod carefully, trying to avoid the ancient graves, and soon reached the building. Next, he needed to find the entrance to the crypt on the west side. He stayed close to the thick walls as he negotiated the uneven ground along the first long wall, hoping that no one would notice him and wonder what the hell he was doing. Finally he turned the corner and arrived at the oldest section of the building away from pedestrian passageway.

At the far end of the wall and down close to the ground he saw a very old door. It was the entrance to the crypt. The door was locked and barred – a metal grid covered the top half, and it was set in a massive stone frame, complete with a pointed Norman arch above the door. A few uneven paving stones led to the crypt entrance and in front of the door the original doorstep was made up of several broken slabs of stone. Underneath one of them he saw a deep crack. He looked around to see if anyone was watching and quickly stuck the green tipped toothpick into the crack until just the green top showed, confident it would only be found by a careful searcher. He straightened up and looked around again – and saw two young boys playing hide and seek among the gravestones, and a little further off a couple putting fresh flowers on a grave. He hoped to God they hadn't been watching, but as the text had instructed, he bent down again and stuck the orange tipped toothpick far into an adjoining crack, in case they had seen him – *"orange if it is possible you were observed, red tipped if it is probable you were observed"* …. He pretended to retie his sneaker before he stood up again and wandered around the old graveyard reading inscriptions on the stones for another ten minutes.

29

I've had enough of reading tombstones to last a lifetime he thought to himself as he left the graveyard behind...

He headed back to his car, dropping the red tipped toothpick in the nearest trash bin, and felt a weight lift off his shoulders....

Sunday the weather closed in again and early afternoon he decided to explore further along the coast and then find somewhere for dinner away from the hotel. He parked his car in one of the lay-bys along the cliff road and scanned the view. The coast reminded him a lot of northern California, the same steep cliffs and rocky inlets, but the movement in and out of the tides seemed much greater than on the Californian coast, and the stretches of sand more expansive. Rocky promontories reached far out into the sea separating wide sandy bays. He had been told that the point on the far side of the next bay was part of the National Trust, and that he should make sure he walked right to the end while he was staying in the area – there were seals in the caves at the base of the cliffs which could only be reached at low tide, by boat or with the help of ropes from above. He made a mental note that they would go there when she got back. He realized that he was missing her and was planning his outings, not so much to re-kindle his boyhood memories but with her in mind, things they would do after she was with him. It gave him pause for thought...

He had dinner that night in a pub-com-roadhouse that he had seen on their way down from London, back on the main road a couple of miles before they had reached the village. Complete with thatched roof and large carpark it attracted the holiday crowd and had been updated and groomed to meet their expectations – with an upscale dining room to match. He elected to eat in the dining room rather than at the bar and had a leisurely meal of "locally grown organic produce", and found the prices upscale too, in line with the rest of the pub.

Dinner over, it was still early and he found himself drawn to the old pub opposite the church. He realized the whole matter of the toothpicks and seeing the man in the pub with the toothpick last weekend had become an obsession with him – and after that additional text last weekend, the *"one small favor"* had taken on a whole new meaning – but he told himself *just this one last time* to convince himself that he was being a fool, and then he'd let it go.

The pub was crowded as usual and he made his way to the bar and ordered a beer.

"Hello!" A voice behind him said. "You're still here, where's your friend?"

He turned and saw the man who had been in the pub picking his teeth with the toothpick the previous weekend – as friendly and inquisitive as ever.

"Yes, I'm still here, my partner had to return to the States, but she'll be back next week." Then he added, "Do you live around here?"

"No, just – two lagers please," the man broke in as he caught the bartenders eye, "visiting. We're waiting for a friend to join us then we move on at the end of the week. We're hiking the Heritage Trail."

The man picked up his beers and started back to his companion.

"Come and join us for a meal if you get bored before your friend gets back, we're saying at the George Hotel."

"Thanks." He replied. "I may take you up on that." – Though he had no intention of ever seeing the man again if he could help it....

"Where are you staying?" The man called back over his shoulder.

Without thinking he gave the man the name of his hotel, wishing afterwards that he hadn't.

He stayed with the crowd around the bar, most of who lived locally, and for the next hour was plied with things to do, local history and local characters until it was time to get back to his hotel.

As he left, he passed by the table where the man and his friends were sitting, noticing that the second friend had arrived and the three men were poring over a map – (*Ah! the Heritage Trail he thought*). He glanced down at the map, but that was not what caught his eye, in front of each man, on the table, in addition to their beer glasses, were four toothpicks, each toothpick snapped in two, and each with a painted top, One blue, one yellow, one green... and one orange.

As he opened the door to leave, the bartender called out, "Good Night! Come again."

He turned and waved and saw the men at the table watching him intently.

31

Monday morning breakfast and his usual waiter was back.

"Did you make it all the way to the estuary on Saturday before the rain started again?"

He told him that he had but had saved exploring the sand dunes for another day.

"You'd better do it fast," the waiter said, "The marines practice landings and bombing runs up there by the estuary several times a year and one's due sometime next week, the front desk can tell you the exact days. They'll be closing off the beach and part of the Burrows up by the estuary when that happens – but you'll get a front row seat from the hotel – it looks like a regular war movie. Older people say it feels like back in the War when our boys and the Americans trained all along these beaches for the invasion of France. No one was allowed anywhere near the beach or the Burrows in those days – there were mines, tank traps and barbed wire everywhere.... More coffee, Sir?"

The waiter left to welcome new arrivals, spreading good cheer and sundry information as he moved between the tables.

He finished his breakfast and decided to find out when the military exercises were due to begin. As he crossed the lounge on his way to the lobby he saw the doorman opening the door for three men, and immediately recognized them from the pub the night before. *What the hell are they doing here?* He slumped down into one of the high-backed armchairs, back to the lobby, out of sight. He hoped they weren't looking to include him in their holiday plans, whatever they might be. It was the last thing he wanted. Cautiously he looked around the back of the chair, feeling foolish and hoping no one was watching, and saw the men wandering around the lobby. One of them pointed to the front desk but another shook his head. They stood by the elevator door for a few minutes and stopped at the bottom of the stairs and looked up towards the mezzanine – and then casually walked out again.

He did not know what to think, weird friends who enjoyed scavenger hunts – just overly friendly – or something more sinister? *What had they got planned for the Heritage Trail he wondered!* Whoever they were, they seemed to be very interested in getting to know him better and this annoyed and disturbed him.

32

After they left he went to the reception desk and learnt that the military exercises would start the following week on Monday, but was warned that the dunes at the estuary end would be swarming with military personnel probably from Wednesday on, getting ready. On impulse he asked if the men who had just left were guests at the hotel, adding that they seemed familiar to him. The woman behind the desk looked at him coldly denying any understanding of what he was talking about, and when he asked to see the guest register, she froze him out completely.

It was already Monday, a couple of days to explore the dunes before the preparations started and today the weather was fine – *God knows what it will be like tomorrow* – so he started off again, running below the high tide mark almost to the estuary before he turned up towards the Burrows running on in the deep dry sand up into the sand dunes.

He climbed until he reached the top of one of the highest dunes and looked around him.

The estuary was close below him and he saw that the tide was coming in, filling the channels and covering the mud flats. A little way in from the shore and just into the dunes he saw the ruin of the old lighthouse and close by, the structure that had been erected to replace it, a huge automatic light built on tall metal stilts looking remarkably like a creature from outer space. As before, several boats were beached on the sand waiting for the tide, or for their owners or both. Further into the Burrows he could make out the warning signs marking the area reserved for the military with a tall flagpole at its highest point. No red flag flying he noted.

He started off towards the area climbing up and down the hot sliding sand with some difficulty, trying to avoid the razor sharp edges of the Pampas Grass planted there to stabilize the dunes. As he got closer to the restricted area he realized what a good location it was – an elevated position with 360° vision of the surrounding area. He could follow the estuary all the way inland to the village and saw how the Burrows sloped down to a narrow strip of sand all the way along the estuary shore. The tide was beginning to come in but mud flats were still visible beyond the sand. *I bet you could walk across to the other side when the tide's right out,* he thought.

His attention was drawn to three men coming down from the Burrows and walking across the sand towards a beached cabin cruiser. One of them pulled himself up onto the deck and disappeared inside the cabin. Shortly he re-appeared lugging a long awkward object. With difficulty he tipped it over the edge of the boat to the other two men waiting there who raised it onto their shoulders and walked towards the ruins of the old lighthouse. The three men were closer now – there was something familiar about them and with mounting disbelief and curiosity – and some apprehension – he realized that they were the same three men who seemed to be dogging his footsteps. One of men looked up and scanned the area and he ducked behind a sand dune hoping to God he hadn't been seen. He watched while they carried the object into the foundations of the old lighthouse and covered it with driftwood. All three of the men scanned the area carefully to make sure they were alone, before turning and heading back along the estuary shore. Once beyond the restricted area they climbed up into the Burrows, and headed inland back towards the village.

He waited in the sand dunes until they were well out of sight then turned and ran back along the wet sand towards the hotel, periodically looking around to see if anyone was watching him... The ocean was a magnet and he ran down close to the edge of the water and soon waded out into the surf, diving through the waves and swimming parallel to the shore out beyond the swells, occasionally body surfing the waves in to the shore. The waves absorbed his thoughts and temporarily he forgot all about work and men with toothpicks.

He returned to his room, showered off the sand and salt, then sat down and sent her a long email, telling her what he had done during the day and what they would do once she was there with him...

Time for a drink and then dinner. He went down to the lounge and sat at the bar. A voice behind him said, "We meet again!"

He turned and faced the same three men.

This is getting ridiculous he thought. "Indeed!" He answered.

"We decided we'd check out where you're slumming," the man said jovially. "Great weather today, did you run on the beach again?"

"Yes – How about you guys?"

"We did, but we were down the other end and came across the Burrows, we saw several people out running and wondered if one of them might be you... Well, we're about to leave, enjoy your dinner."
"Thanks." He replied.
He waited to make sure that they had really left, then went to the reception desk and inquired if anyone had been asking about him. This time there was a man behind the desk. He replied in the negative.
"If anyone does, please do not give out any information about my being here, and please do not give out my room number."
"As I know you are aware, Sir, it is not our policy to give out room numbers or any other information about our guests."
The atmosphere had turned to ice again. He marveled how quickly and efficiently the staff had been trained to end difficult conversations. They could turn on a dime and freeze out even the most insistent guest he suspected.
Back in his room he sent her several texts. *They're back. Up to something in the dunes! Showed up again in the bar. You still think I'm paranoid?* Tomorrow he decided he would write everything down, maybe it would help him organize his thoughts so they made sense....

Tuesday it was raining again and he settled in to grapple with his thoughts. But it wasn't that easy .... *Where should he start? With that stupid toothpick? Nobody would take that seriously - but maybe that was just the point – everyone, including himself, had thought it a joke, and it might be just that .... But then there was the man who had contacted him in New York – was he one of the men here now? Somehow he doubted that .... Maybe the toothpick was a signal that they were ready for the next stage .... What next stage? – Maybe the personal ad was part of the message too? Now he really was being paranoid.... It had started with just one man with an "innocent request" – help with a harmless "favor" – Damn! How gullible he had been, he'd been sucked in so easily! Now there were at least three of them, and probably others, maybe a whole network?....*
And then there was the talkative one, he'd always been friendly – too much so to his mind, it had made him uneasy .... *Was there an ulterior motive, where they watching him? Why? Because of the toothpick? That*

35

was crazy! – Or because he knew who they were now? So what were they up to?.... Maybe they were just hiking the Heritage trail as they had told him in the pub – the Burrows had trails that were part of the Coastal Path... Last night the man had asked if he had run on the beach "again". How did he know that he had run on the beach the day before? –Had they been watching him from the beginning?.... What about the boat? What was that object they removed from it and hid in the old lighthouse? His paranoid Self told him it was a shoulder missile launcher – especially with the Marine training exercise about to start... His other Self told him not to be stupid, it was just fishing gear. *Should he tell someone his concerns? .... Was he being paranoid?*

He didn't even know which Self to listen to. He felt no further forward. He realized that even if he decided to go to the authorities he had absolutely no proof of anything irregular. What could he tell them? That he saw three friends hiking the Coastal Path, making it more interesting by searching for – *toothpicks?* It sounded crazy even to him. And he had no proof of his suspicions. Not even a broken toothpick. They would think he was crazy. And maybe he was…….

Enough! He needed to get out. Maybe a drive would help to clear his head.

He drove through the village and five miles on, through the old market town on the banks of one of the two rivers that merged into the estuary before flowing out to sea. He had found the town changed – not for the better – spoilt by modern day traffic patterns which did not exist when he had visited as a boy. He was glad when he saw a few remnants of its medieval roots still standing.

He crossed the old bridge spanning the river and drove up the hill past the train station – where he would meet her on Saturday – and on along the main coast road on the other side of the estuary, to the twin market town on the second river. He was happy to find this town less changed, the medieval quay now had places to park cars, but the old town itself, built into the steep hills, still had its narrow vertical streets, and although a second bridge had been built on the bypass just outside the town, the medieval bridge spanning the river was still very much in use. He crossed it and drove through the town and on to the fishing village almost directly across the estuary from where he was staying.

36

He got out and walked along the quay. Across the water he could see his hotel with the cliffs and rocks beyond it, and the Burrows leading back towards the village. He realized how different the two sides of the estuary were. Across from where he was standing it was more rural, and apart from the cliffs on the promontory, flatter. The shore sloped gradually to the water and he saw that the village - the church spire prominent – was in the estuary flood plain, hills rising up behind it. It was very different from where he was standing, where the land dropped off sharply with deep water harbors at high-tide and boats tied up against granite quays.

He walked around the village for a while, stopped for a pub lunch at the local watering hole and then got back in his car and turned around to go back the way he had come. Once on the other side of the estuary again he found a police station.

"Can I help you, Sir?" from the policeman behind the counter.

"I don't know," He replied. He told him where he was staying. "It is probably nothing, but yesterday I went for a run along the beach and ran up into the dunes where I could see the estuary, and I saw three men walk up to a cabin cruiser beached there and one of them climbed up into the boat, went into the cabin and came back pulling a long object which he heaved up over the side of the deck to the other two men who caught it and took it into the old lighthouse ruins. I don't know if the boat belonged to them, or if they were stealing something or what, but I thought I should tell you what I saw."

The police man asked, "You didn't mention this to anyone when you got back to the hotel?"

"No, it didn't seem that significant then but I got to thinking about it today. That's why I'm here. I don't know, I know the Marines are having one of their training exercises on the beach next Monday and I had this weird thought just now that it might have been a shoulder missile launcher that I saw them carrying."

The policeman thanked him, and replied that it wasn't under their jurisdiction but he would make sure the information was passed on to the correct authorities.

Now he had voiced his concerns the policeman's reply made him anxious. "Please make sure it's checked out as soon as possible, next Monday is coming up fast!"

The policeman assured him that it was in good hands and would be passed on, asked for his contact information and bid him "Good afternoon."

He left the police station unsettled. He was relieved that he had told someone – at least part of the story – but he had the feeling that there was no urgency to check out his information. He hoped he was misinterpreting... Maybe if he had told the whole story? No, he felt, with nothing to back it up that would have made it worse, he had done what he could, *let it go...*

Wednesday he woke up wishing she was there with him. Time was dragging, he had been counting the days to Saturday, but it was still three days away. He needed her sane philosophy of life to help him sort out all his crazy thoughts.

Thoughts of men and toothpicks crowded his head once again and he needed to get out and do something different to clear his mind. So after breakfast he set off to hike around the next headland and across the next bay to the Point owned by the National Trust. He had learnt that the Point was also part of the Southwest Coastal Path winding its way along the coasts of Devon and Cornwall, and part of the network of Heritage Trails going all around England.

He headed north out of his hotel onto the headland path on the edge of the cliffs. For the first two miles it was easy going, but then the path petered out and he was forced to climb down onto the rocks below, jumping from one rock to the next looking for footholds. It was another hour before he finally reached the firm sand of the next bay. It had taken him longer than he had expected to hike over the headland to where he was standing.

He stopped and stretched and looked around him, and saw almost the mirror image of his beach. Behind him, the way he had come, the cliff towered above the rocky terrain at its base. In front of him, large waves surged onto a long stretch of sand reaching out to the distant Point. There the similarity ended, at the far end of the bay were many more signs of civilization. Small hotels and large holiday houses dotted the cliff-top out to the beginning of the Point.

He walked along the edge of the sea in the shallow water to the far end of the bay, then took the path between the sand dunes up off the beach until it turned into a tarmacked road, complete with a bench, and a board posting bus timetables. Off to one side, a large carpark. He looked at the timetable, and saw that the buses stopped in front of his hotel. He figured it might be useful at the end of the day after he had hiked around the Point.

With that in mind he decided he didn't have to worry about sunset, and set off along the road away from the Point the short distance to the local village to find a pub for lunch before he continued on with his hike. After his lunch he wandered through the small village finding it picturesque but filled with tourists. It wasn't long before he was on his way along the road back towards the Point – but it was a couple of miles more before he was clear of the bed and breakfasts and holiday camps dotted along the road. Finally, after passing a few magnificent homes facing out to sea, he reached the National Trust Carpark marking the beginning of the Point.

The promontory that formed the Point was much wider than he had realized when he had looked at it from the beach. At first low hills rose gradually up and over to the other side and he saw what looked like a farmhouse half hidden in the distance. A signpost directed him to the Southwest Coastal Path and he started off along a wide dusty path well away from the cliff edge. A famous walled garden on the main path offered admission, but he was not in the mood for flowers today – maybe after she arrived they would come back and take their time to smell the roses...

Soon he was on the smaller path which ran along the edge of the cliffs facing the bay he had crossed earlier in the day. The terrain changed again and the path to the point became narrower – cut into a steep hill on one side and treacherously close to the edge on the other. All the way along the Point at the base of the cliffs the waves pounded onto formidable granite rocks. The sound of the surf breaking onto the rocks and the warm sun was relaxing him.

Near the end of the land the Coastal Path curved around, a signpost directing him to follow the bend along the other side of the promontory. Directly in front of him a narrow trail continued down and seemed to go right to the very end of the Point. It dropped down sharply, parts of it worn away and at the end he could see a rope cordoning off a small plateau of turf going right to the edge of the cliffs. Another sign at the beginning of this trail warned of difficult terrain, uneven footing, and possible landslides.

He figured it was only about two hundred feet to the end, but it was a long way down if he slipped. The trail looked pretty stable to him, and the weather was perfect... Far below he could hear the surf crashing onto the rocks at the bottom of the cliffs. The sound was continuous – deafening – rhythmic – hypnotic. He climbed down, trying to avoid the places where the sandstone cliff had started to fall away and reached the end of the trail without incident. At the end, attached to the rope, he read another sign.

End of Trail
WARNING!
No one allowed beyond this point
Unstable! Keep Away From Edge

From where he was standing he had a fantastic view of the waves rolling into an inlet far below. They surged in, one following after another, the swells growing to a monstrous size then crashing against the jagged rocks at the base of the cliff, the surf throwing foam and spray high into the air. He wondered if the inlet led to the seal caves and he toyed with the idea of going to the other side of the rope where would be able to see the inlet from a different angle.

He looked around. Way out at sea a small launch was travelling parallel to the shore and he wondered casually where it was heading.

Then he looked back the way he had come and saw three men coming single file down the narrow trail towards him.

Even from where he stood he recognized them – he hoped they could not see him, but knew that that was a futile hope. Their walk was purposeful, one behind the other keeping straight on down the trail towards him. Yes, they had seen him all right but their friendliness had gone…. no calling out to him, no talking to each other, and now they were closer he saw no expression on their faces. He was trapped. The sign he had just read flashed through his mind … *Fuck! …What now?* …

Suddenly he was frightened. There was no way he could pass them on the narrow trail to get back to the Coastal Path, and the relentless way they kept on coming was menacing.

He was cornered, the only way was down... Maybe there would be foothold in the cliff below him... Maybe he could make it down to a ledge.... Maybe that boat would see him and pick him up. *What other option did he have?* He jumped the rope and went to the edge of the cliff. He saw a perilous drop – off to his left and about twelve feet down there was a very small ledge in the cliff, maybe he could reach it... *then what?...* where was the next foothold?

He looked back, they were still coming on down the trail, one behind the other, in lockstep, same pace, no slowing, no rushing, no stopping. He looked over the edge again. The noise of the waves surging onto the rocks was deafening and for a moment mesmerized him. He looked back again. The lead man was almost at the end of the trail. He turned back and again looked over the edge, looking for footholds, fighting vertigo – and felt hands on his back push him forward.

He fell out from the edge a long way down, nothing to break his fall except the rocks at the bottom of the cliff stretching far out into the sea.

The next wave surged in, white fingers of surf pouring into the crevices of the rocks, swirling around, washing the body, retreating out into open sea again. Another followed, and another, and another, they surged in and out relentlessly.

No sound except the seagulls and the waves.

Far out at sea the boat continued on its way.

FIVE

Three days later she arrived back in the UK. Her flight had been uneventful but long and she had not slept. She felt unsettled – really looking forward to their vacation but wondering why he had not been texting her recently – she figured he was hiking out in the wilds somewhere without Wi-Fi – and hoped that it was not some slick chick on the beach who was keeping him occupied..... Jealous thoughts rarely occurred to her, both of them had purposefully placed limits on the relationship and it had been working as well for her as it had been for him, but after the last two weeks apart she was beginning to think that there was a subtle change and that maybe they were getting more committed to each other long term. *That's funny,* she thought – *it's already been two years.*

It was very early on Saturday morning and the first thing she did was find a large cup of strong black coffee. She texted him that she had arrived – still no answer – but the caffeine revived. She quickly found the entrance to Heathrow Express and took the tube to Paddington Station – the hub for travel to the west of England. Paddington, she found was huge and confusing and it took her precious minutes to find the correct Great Western platform for her train to the Southwest. She was travelling light not wanting to lug suitcases on and off trains, and was glad she was because in the end she had to rush to make the train to Exeter.

An hour and a half later the train arrived at Exeter-St. David's Station where she had to change onto the local train. But then her journey slowed to a crawl. Frustrated, she found she had to wait almost two hours for her connection to North Devon. Her train eventually pulled into the platform and she settled herself in a window seat. And waited another ten minutes before they finally started to move ... She found her impatience increasing as it meandered through Devon, lingering at the many small descriptively named stations along the way.....

Five hours after leaving London she arrived at the end of the line and got off the train.

She had expected him to be on the platform to meet her and was surprised and upset that he wasn't there – he had sounded so eager for her to join him when she had told him her travel plans the previous weekend, and again her uneasiness at him not answering any of her texts for the past few days bubbled up inside her. She quashed them again, remembering how bad mobile service was in most of the southwest. Taxis were waiting outside the station and she got in the one at the head of the line, giving the driver the address of the hotel on the cliffs on the North Devon coast where they were staying. Once in the cab she tried texting him again – but again there was no reply. It was summer holiday season and the ten-mile taxi ride took longer than normal but eventually she arrived at the hotel where a liveried doorman opened the cab door and welcomed her to the hotel, a little disdainful at her lack of meaningful luggage when he saw just one carryon suitcase.

At the front desk she gave his name and room number and asked that he be paged. The man behind the desk asked her to please wait one moment, and disappeared, she presumed to call his room. Very quickly he returned, followed by another man who he introduced as the manager of the hotel.

They shook hands.

"Would you follow me, please?"

Now bewildered she did as he asked and found herself in his well-appointed office.

He directed her to a chair. "Was he expecting you?"

"Yes, I believe both our names are on the reservation. We made the reservation two weeks ago and I finalized my arrival plans last weekend. I flew in this morning. He knew I was going to take the train down to Devon but I was surprised that he wasn't at the station to meet me...."

"Did you reach him?" She turned to the second man as he came back into the room. "Did he say where he was?"

The second man glanced towards the manager and did not answer.

The manager, looked very uncomfortable. "I'm very sorry to have to tell you that your friend is dead."

She went blank – then a thousand emotions welled up inside her – total disbelief – an overwhelming sense of loss and grief – fear because of what had been going on – but above everything else a gnawing ache that she had not been with him.

The manager let her sit there silently for several minutes then continued.

"His body was found on the rocks below the cliffs on the Point. They think he fell or jumped from the cliffs."

"What do you mean jumped?" She said angrily. "He would never, never have jumped, he loved life, killing himself was not in his nature."

"The cliffs are very steep in that area and some tourists these days try to climb down to the caves, so he probably fell." He answered, trying to comfort her.

"When did it happen?"

"His body was found Wednesday evening by a young couple watching the sunset. Naturally, we notified the authorities at once. The coroner interviewed the staff and recorded death from undetermined causes, either accidental or by his own hand."

"It wasn't suicide! Why was that even suggested?"

The manager looked embarrassed. "When they were questioned, some of the staff reported that he was acting strangely and seemed nervous. One reported him hiding in a storage closet. He was always looking around to see if anyone was following him. Frankly we thought he seemed a little paranoid. He even came to the front desk one time, asking to see the guest register. Naturally we did not agree to his request..." He went on – "Of course, now I realize he was looking to see if his sister and her husband had arrived."

She jerked up straight in her chair. "His sister?" "I didn't …" suddenly caution welled up and she changed what she was going to say in mid-sentence, "know she was coming."

Before their conversation at Heathrow she had been sure he did not have a sister – or a brother, and that both his parents were dead, but now she didn't know anything. *What else hadn't he told her?*

Very quietly she added, "I want to see him, where is he? Can you tell me how to get there?"

The manager looked even more uncomfortable.

"His sister and her husband arrived Thursday, the morning after his body had been found. They came to the desk and asked for him – just as you did – apparently they had been planning to meet up at the hotel that same day. His sister was distraught when she heard what had happened and wanted to get his body back home to the States as soon as possible. We put her in touch with the authorities and she identified his body."

She asked again where his body was so she could see him, and the manager reluctantly told her that the coroner had not felt that an autopsy was necessary and Friday morning had released his body to his sister who had got permission to have him cremated. Cremation, the manager said he had been told, was usual when the deceased had to be transported back to another country. And he understood they were going to fly back to the States this weekend.

It was unbelievable to her; she could not sort it out in her head…. what had happened? *Who was this "sister" What had they got involved in –* One thing she knew for certain, it was all because of that one obscene "small favor" he had carried out for some unknown obscene being.

"What happened to his things, did they take them with them?" She asked. *She needed a connection to him – something to hold onto, something tangible.*

"Actually, no," the manager replied. "His sister was too upset to think about it, but I took her husband up to the room – he looked around briefly and I think he took his mobile, but not much else. He asked if we could store the rest until he could arrange to have them sent back to the States. As the room is paid for through next Saturday, I made the decision to leave the room as it is until then – your friend had

45

mentioned that he was expecting you to be joining him for the second week, so the room is yours this week, if it's not too painful for you."

She tried to focus, fighting nausea and the buzzing in her head.

"I really can't think what my plans are right now, but I will stay, at least for tonight, and you don't have to store his things, I'll take them with me when I leave. Can you take me to the room now please?"

"Of course," he replied. "Can I get you anything, a drink?" "Some tea?"

She shook her head, "I don't know, I can't think, I just want to go to our room."

The manager accompanied her to their room in the front of the hotel overlooking the sea.

"I expect you would like to be alone." He said. "But I am going to send up something for you to eat, and also new key cards for your door."

She thanked him. As he closed the door he saw her standing at the window staring out at the ocean.

She waited until the manager had gone then went over and double locked the door. She had to get her thoughts together. *How could he be dead?* She knew he hadn't killed himself, and she was sure that he had not fallen off the cliffs – though that would have been slightly more credible if it hadn't been for the phony sister and her phony husband showing up. *Why hadn't she told the manager that the sister was a fake, why had she kept it to herself?*

There was a knock on the door and a voice called out.

"Room service."

She opened the door and a waiter pushed the trolley into the room and set it up for her – tea and coffee, sandwiches and fruit.

"The compliments of the Manager, Miss. He didn't know if you would prefer tea or coffee, so he sent both."

She thanked him, scanned the room to see where she had dropped her bag, found some money, tipped him, and he left.

She was exhausted and knew she was thinking around in circles, making no sense. She poured a cup of tea, but put it down untouched, then picked up a ham sandwich and nibbled at the edge before she put that down too, feeling sick all over again. She lay down on the bed – and smelt the anonymous aroma of fresh sheets – no lingering scent of him

46

which would have made her break down completely but would have been comforting and would have grounded her. She had no bearings. She felt she was in a dense cloud, voices sounded far away and floated in and out of the constant buzzing in her head. *He couldn't be dead...* She closed her eyes and slept, curled up in a ball.

It was almost dark when she woke and she could hear the sound of the waves pounding on the beach below the cliff. She automatically reached out for him and found only the empty bed. *Oh God! They told me he was dead...* The buzzing in her head had receded and she lay on the bed immobile, looking up at the ceiling, thinking. *He's dead... He can't be!... What should she do? What needed to be done? Was he really dead?... Why had he died? Why hadn't the hotel tried to reach her on Thursday – probably because that damn phony sister and husband had shown up... Who were those people, where had they come from? She was sure there was no half-sister, she would have known.... What had they done with his ashes? She was sure they would not have taken them back to the States. Had they really left England? Where they still around checking on her? If they had his mobile they would know all about her and when she would arrive. She had to be careful...* She sat up on the bed, and looked around the room, deciding the first thing she needed to do was search to see what was there. She picked up one of the now stale sandwiches from the trolley suddenly realizing how hungry she was. The coffee at Heathrow Airport early that morning was the only thing she'd had all day and she vaguely wondered what the time was now.

She started to search the room. A few clothes in the closet, the same for the chest of drawers, only hotel information in the bedside tables, and only toilet articles in the bathroom. Nothing out of the ordinary – but seeing and touching his things tore her apart. She found his briefcase in the bottom of the closet and took it to the bed to go through it. She found nothing out of the ordinary there either – only reports from the meetings he had attended and a list of possible acquisitions he was researching for his company – nothing more. She wondered if he had brought his laptop to England, because that was not in the case, and she realized that his Blackberry, which he kept exclusively for business, was not there either – so his Blackberry was missing, was that the only phone the man had taken? Then where was his personal mobile? Did he have it with him when he was killed? – In that case, she thought, it might have been swept away by the waves. Just *maybe* they didn't know everything he had told her, or even when she was arriving…. She put his briefcase back in the closet and went through the pockets of his clothes more carefully, finding nothing. She suddenly remembered the car, where was it? And where were the keys. She wondered if the man had taken them – She wished she knew what he had taken from the room.

By the time she had finished it was totally dark. She left the room and went down through the lounge where a few guests and staff still lingering around the bar – and out onto the patio, down onto the lawn. Discrete lighting guided her across the grass and down the steps cut into the cliff onto the deserted beach. The sand above the high-tide mark, so hot during the day was now ice cold and damp beneath her feet, the surf luminous in the moonlight, the sound of the waves relentless in the background. She walked along the sand for a while then sat down facing the sea hugging her knees and watched the waves, longing for him to be there with her.

Hours later she got up from the damp sand, chilled through and stiff. The sea was much closer now and she headed back towards the hotel. As she passed the path leading up to the carpark she thought she saw a man in the shadows of the dunes watching the beach. She shook off the thought that he was watching her and hurried up the cliff steps back to the hotel. Once back in her room she took a long hot shower then climbed back on the bed and once more fell asleep.

SIX

She was woken up by the sound of voices in the corridor outside her room, the hotel was wide awake and the clock beside her bed told her it was well past nine o'clock. For a moment she could not remember where she was or what was happening, then it all came roaring back. She sat down suddenly on the bed the wind knocked out of her, nauseous all over again.

"Focus!" She said out loud.

She stood up, gritted her teeth, got dressed and went down for breakfast.

The waiter came over to take her order then hesitated before speaking. "I was so sorry to hear about your friend, he was a very nice man, and we had some good conversations, my condolences."

She put down her coffee. "Do you think he killed himself? Apparently some of the staff thought he was paranoid."

"Personally, I thought he was as sane as you and me." He answered. "I would not have thought that it would cross his mind – besides he was looking forward to you arriving to join him, that's why he went to the Point, to check it out for when you got here."

"So what do you think happened?" She questioned.

"The cliffs on the Point are very dangerous, I can't imagine him going that close to the edge – he seemed very sensible, but that's what he probably did, I suppose."

A couple at a table across the room caught the waiters' eye and he backed away from her table to find out what they needed.

As she drank her coffee she thought about what she should do next. She needed to find out what had really happened, she needed a plan....

First she had to find their car. She remembered the color and make and had learnt from previous hard experience always to memorize the license plate number. She finished her breakfast quickly and went out into the lobby where she was directed to the guest carpark by the doorman. "Outside and down to the left."

It did not take her long to locate their car but found it locked, as she figured she would. Inside she could see his windbreaker, a guide book on the local area and a half finished bottle of water, nothing more. She cursed the rental company for only giving out one set of keys and supposed that meant she would have to call to get duplicates. She knew the rental agreement was in the glove compartment, and again, she realized that without the details she had no proof that the car was rented to her. She figured that would mean a long and arduous automated call. *No hope of getting an actual voice on the phone on a Sunday, she thought.*

Frustration was already bubbling to the surface and she wished she was as calm as he had always been. What would he do? *Go for a run she told herself.* Back in the lobby she saw a notice informing the guests of the military exercises that would take place the next day. The woman at the front desk told her that she could still run on the beach today, but that there seemed to be more restrictions than usual when one of these exercises was about to take place, and that she would not be able to go as far as the estuary.

"You may be stopped and questioned." The woman told her. "They don't usually do that, but they seem much more thorough than last time, and there are many more of them. Sign of the times I suppose."

She changed into shorts and a tee and took off along the beach.

Near the end of the sands she climbed up into the dunes and as the woman at the front desk had warned her, was stopped and questioned – Where was she from? How long she had been at the hotel? And how long did she intend to stay? The run had helped her to relax, but the soldier's questioning made her tense again. She answered him

50

concisely. She knew that if she said anything about past incidents it would mean a lengthy interrogation and she felt too emotionally exhausted to go into everything that had happened recently in their lives – besides it probably had no relevance. And she had no evidence, no proof of anything – except for one of the last texts she had received from him which had told her about the men and the boat in the estuary, and that, he had told her, he had reported it to the authorities. It was no point bringing up something they already knew about. Being questioned by the soldier helped her think, and she decided to drive the eight miles into the town the next day to talk with the coroner and the police, and she felt that then would be a better time to explain her fears and try to explain what had been going on.

So she missed an opportunity to talk.

But now she had a plan. She ran back to the hotel and went up to the room to shower. The first thing she needed to do was to get keys for the car. It suddenly occurred to her that he might have used the hotel's valet parking in which case they would have the keys. She phoned the bellman. No luck, no keys – he had parked the car himself.

If he was that concerned that the three men were following him, he might have hidden them, she thought. She'd already searched the room thoroughly, but now she took it apart. She felt between the mattress and box spring – under the edges of the carpet – under the lamps – she pulled out all the drawers and looked behind and under them – felt on top of the window frames – practically took the back off the television – everywhere in the closet... No luck. She started on the bathroom – in and behind the commode tank –behind the toilet roll holder – behind and in the tissue box... No luck. Discouraged, she went out into the bedroom again and sat on the bed looking around to see what she had missed. The refrigerator – she needed a drink anyway.... She took the bottles and cans out one by one and right at the back, under a can of ginger ale found the keys. Thank God! He'd saved them for her. She poured herself a scotch and toasted him silently, then took her drink to the window and looked out at the ocean, wishing he was there with her, trying to believe that he was actually dead, tears rolling down her face as she finished her drink.

51

She knew she was falling apart. It was as if he had been vaporized, nothing of him remained, no closure, no goodbyes, nothing remained, nor even his ashes. She felt very alone but could not face anyone. For the rest of the day she stayed curled up on the bed, overwhelmed, feeling lost and totally abandoned. She drifted in and out of sleep and it was evening before she woke up enough to think.

She was not hungry but self-preservation told her she needed to eat something so she ordered room service and when the food arrived forced herself to eat a few mouthfuls. Everything tasted like cardboard, but it helped her to re-focus and she spent the next few hours on her mobile –looking up UK law, local information, the location of the coroner's office, the crematorium – and the addresses of the police stations around the town where he might have reported what he had seen in the estuary. She planned to visit them all until she found the correct one.

SEVEN

The following morning she was up early, anxious to put her plan into action. The beach had been closed for the military exercises and many of the guests were already staking out their place on the patio so they would have a front row seat to watch the planes practicing landings and vertical take-offs.

After a quick breakfast she went to the front entrance and out to the guest parking lot. The car was as she remembered it from the day before, but this time she had the keys and could get inside. It was disturbing to find his things where he had left them the last time he had driven the car – the half-finished bottle of water somehow the hardest to take. She unscrewed the cap and gave in to the urge to drink the water. She was anxious to hit the road so searched the car quickly finding nothing to add to the meager information she already had, and made a mental note to check it out more thoroughly later. It was still early and there was not much traffic on the road except for a convoy of military vehicles, on their way to the beach she surmised. Normally she would have enjoyed the drive. Once past the village the road ran along the side of the estuary and this time the tide was going out – she figured the marines would not be practicing their landings until low tide – and wondered how long the exercises lasted. Five miles on she reached the market town.

She had decided to wait until after she had been to the police station to go to the coroner's office, so first she set off to visit all the police stations in town until she found the one he had gone to. It did not take very long. She had purposely started on the far end of town, correctly thinking that once he came back over the bridge from his trip to the other side of the estuary he would go to the first one he saw. Almost correct, it took her three tries before she found the right one, but then she had some luck. The policeman who he had talked to that day was on duty, and the desk clerk called him to the front to speak to her. The policeman told her that her "friend" had reported three men taking a long object off a cabin cruiser beached at the mouth of the estuary, and that he was concerned it might have something to do with the military exercises. "I told him that it was not in our jurisdiction but we would pass it on," the policeman added.

"Who did you pass it on to?"

"To the military, Miss, that seemed to be your friend's main concern."

"Did you hear anything back?"

"No Miss, but we didn't expect to, but they did get the information from us." Then he added, "My condolences about your friend, Miss."

She had not realized that the policeman would know about her partner's death and it threw her.

"Do you think his death had anything to do with what he saw? He had a couple of strangers coming up to him after he had been on the dunes, trying to get to know him. Could it all be connected?"

She knew she was not explaining things well and was not surprised when the policeman told her he did not think there was any connection. "And he probably just slipped while he was climbing down he cliffs." He said sympathetically.

She tried one more time, "Did they find the men?"

"We also called the village police department with the information, but as far as we know they did not find anyone – but the boat could have belonged to them, and if that was the case they weren't doing anything illegal."

She gave up. She knew she was getting nowhere, so thanked him for his help, and left.

She was depressed, every minute of the day she was fighting her loss and trying to stay in the present – and the frustration of no one believing her was adding to her exhaustion.

54

She had to make sense of his death. From the first moment she had heard he was dead she knew he had not killed himself, and by the second day she had totally dismissed the accidental fall theory. She knew he had been killed – *you only had to read his messages to figure that out. Why couldn't she get anyone to listen to her and investigate what happened?*

She needed to find out why he had been killed. She had to make sense of his death for herself, but also she needed everyone to know why he was dead. To the world his death was already in the past and she was just the mourning partner trying to justify why he had "killed himself" *or "just maybe" had fallen from the cliffs? – She could tell from their eyes and their sympathy what they really thought.* She was afraid that like him, she was in danger of being tagged as paranoid. *"Americans, they find a conspiracy everywhere..." She could hear them saying.* She wished she was back in the States. She did not understand the laws – or the people – in this country.

By now it was late morning and she decided to take a break – nobody would be around at lunch time anyway she thought, but first she called the coroner's office, asked the woman who answered for an appointment to see the coroner and explained that she was the partner of the man who had been found at the bottom of the cliffs off the Point last Wednesday – she had some questions she needed answered. The woman said the coroner had some time at 2:00 and gave her directions to the office.

That meant she had two hours to kill. She drove towards the center of the town where she found a hodgepodge of narrow medieval streets – mainly now reserved for pedestrians – and multiple one way streets, barriers and bypasses trying to divert traffic away from the center. Eventually she found a modern three story garage squashed in between a warren of still existing narrow old streets and a new bus and coach terminal, and parked the car. She thought what a terrible mess they had made trying to bring the old town up to "modern day standards." She could just about make out the bones of the beautiful medieval market town it had once been.

She walked up the old high street – now for foot traffic only – and came to the large pannier market, still active. A sign told her that Friday was market day when the farmers would bring in their produce to sell. She walked the length of it, but this was Monday and only a few stalls were open – mainly trinkets, antiques and paperback books. She left through one of the tall doors at the other end and found herself on an old guild street, the panier market on one side and a row of small shops on the other. She crossed the street and wandered back towards the high street looking into the shops, originally all butcher shops, now fish mongers, greengrocers and bake shops interspersed with the meat, the products in front displays close to the street, open to the customers. Back on the high street she saw a genuine old Tudor building, complete with dark oak cross beams on the outside and the second story jutting out over the street. A hanging sign proudly announced it was a pub, and had been for the last four hundred years. She decided to go there for lunch. Loud music, neon and the smell of pizza greeted her as she entered and she fled back to the street. She finished up buying one of the local pasties from a bake shop and by then it was time to head back to go to the coroner's office.

After the mess she felt she had made trying to explain what had happened to the policeman earlier that morning she was determined to tell her story logically and without emotion this time around. She would go right back to the beginning and tell everything...
The coroner turned out to be a medical man – older, a little tubby and very friendly – with an aura of patronizing sympathy.
After the usual offer of condolences, he directed her to the chair across from his desk. He took his seat and asked her what questions he could answer for her. She launched into her story – starting from the beginning, the ad in the paper several months before, and how they thought it was a joke someone was playing on a friend or a scavenger hunt or something, and as he was going to be in England at that time anyway....
He broke in "Where you going with him?"
"Not originally, it was a business trip, but then he started to get more texts and started to worry about what he had got himself into and I suggested that I go with him and we could have a vacation together after he'd placed he toothpick."

"He didn't think to back out? This all sounds very strange." He said.

"He did, but by then he was intrigued and couldn't let go." She replied.

The coroner continued "Did you actually see him place the toothpick?"

"No, he dropped me off at the beach first, but he said everything went smoothly when he got back."

She continued with her story and he listened patiently although she had the distinct feeling he had already made up his mind that what she was trying to tell him had nothing to do with her partner's death and he was just humoring her. She told how he had seen the man at the bar picking his teeth with the blue-tipped toothpick (cringing to herself at how totally bizarre it sounded) and went on to recount how he had texted her after she had returned to the States when he had seen the same man with two other men in the same pub with broken color-tipped toothpicks on their table; and about all the other texts he had sent telling about how the men were always showing up and he thought they were following him; and about one of the final texts she had received when he told her he had seen the three men entering the beached cabin cruiser at the mouth of the estuary.

The coroner stopped her again.

"From what you've told me, you never actually saw the toothpicks, or the men, right?"

With a start she realized that that was true... She pulled out her phone and scrolled to the long email he had sent her on Tuesday.

"Here, read this – he wrote me about everything that had been going on; about placing the other two toothpicks and seeing them on the table where the three men were sitting in the pub the next day; and that he thought there was significance in the area within the triangle formed by the three locations where he had placed the toothpicks. Someone should check it out!" She urged, "It's the least you can do."

He scanned the message briefly.

"This only confirms what you've already told me, there's nothing new here. Maybe he was playing a joke on you, maybe he was trying to get you to come here with him."

She denied it vehemently. "That makes no sense, I was coming anyway – and you didn't see how upset he was."

She could have bitten her tongue – realizing too late that would make him look as paranoid as people had said.

At the end of her story he leaned forward across his desk and spoke to her gently.

"I don't see how there could be any connection, my dear. Do you think it's just possible he was imagining that the men were following him, and after all, you never actually saw any of this, did you?"

She lost it… "You think he was imagining all his and that he killed himself! He was the sanest man I ever met I tell you those men killed him! I told you what really happened, they killed him!"

"Unfortunately, there is nothing to substantiate anything you've just told me," he said kindly, "I know it's hard to believe but you will get past all this…"

"I haven't finished, there's more." She pulled herself together and continued calmly, "Who was that woman who claimed to be his sister, He didn't have a sister, so who was she? Don't you think it was strange that she and her *husband* showed up so conveniently?"

His patience was beginning to wane, and now she was challenging his actions.

"My Dear, they showed me documents proving who they were, I would never have released his body without their documentation – which we checked thoroughly, by the way."

"But he – did –not –have – a – sister! I know that for a fact."

"My Dear, maybe he just didn't tell you everything. You know men and women don't always share everything with each other…."

He had hit a nerve. With a start she realized that he was right, *maybe there was a half-sister …* She dismissed the thought – *but not one he was aware of; of that she was sure?*

"You are wrong." She said quietly. "You need to double check their papers."

She knew the interview was over and he had not been swayed by anything she had said. She got up from her chair and he came around the desk to say goodbye.

As he ushered her towards the door he put a fatherly arm around her shoulders.

"I know how hard this must be for you, but you will get through this."
He said soothingly.

Closed minded patronizing bastard, she thought. But she gave him a demure "Thank you" as he opened the door for her.

In response he added. "I will go over everything again with what you've just told me."

No you won't, you smooth old phony, you're just trying to fob me off.
She knew he wouldn't, it would challenge his past actions and besides he knew she would be back in the States by the end of the week...
But she thanked him anyway.

She left the coroner's office angry. He had been her best hope and all he had done was try to pacify her and defend his own actions. He had not listened to what she was telling him at all. Her frustrations grew as she went back to get the car.

Her next stop was the crematorium and she was not hopeful that she would learn anything new there, but she had to try. The crematorium was the other side of the bridge, high up on a hill and the visit did not go well. She had expected at least someone who was used to dealing with death and people under stress – instead she got an ill-tempered middle-aged woman who had obviously had a bad day.

She explained to the woman who she was and that she was looking for explanations and was quickly told that as she was just a friend, she had no legal right to their records and that his sister had signed off on everything and had collected his ashes. Foolishly she blurted out that he didn't have a sister which was one of the reasons she was there.

"Men don't always tell their girlfriends everything." The woman replied curtly. "What was his sister's married name? I'll check the particulars."

"I just told you, he didn't have a sister and I have no idea what phony name she was using," she said, having a hard time to keep her voice and anger under control, "Can you at least give me the date when this happened?"

All in one tired breath the woman replied. "The cremation was Thursday, they picked the ashes up Friday morning, they said they were flying out in the afternoon, I don't know where to, they had the certificate from the crematorium for the ashes, we are not required to give documentation for the airlines – if that's your next question – and also I have no idea if they or the ashes actually flew out. Anything else?" *You really are a first class bitch, she thought.*

"Thank you for your help." She said sarcastically as she left.

.... And had the sudden insight that the woman was probably thinking exactly the same about her...

She got back in the car and headed down the hill and across the bridge, wanting to leave the town behind as quickly as possible. She figured that one quick left- hand turn off the bridge would get her back on the road to the hotel, but found she was not allowed to turn there. Instead she had to wind her way through the narrow streets, all the time fighting to control her frustrations at the utter uselessness of her day, and her terrible sadness. It took her another fifteen minutes to find the correct road back to the coast on the other side of the town.

Though actually she was in no hurry. For the first time in her life she had no idea what to do next. It had been a very depressing day, and she was beginning to lose hope that anyone would listen, let alone believe her story – or that there was even a remote possibility that anyone would ever investigate what she was trying to tell them. Would she ever find out what really happened? *What difference would it make, he still wouldn't be there with her, it wouldn't change anything ... Would it really make a difference if she knew what happened? .... Yes it would! For him, and for her, that's why she couldn't let it go... She had to make someone care....*

Her head buzzed with jumbled thoughts as she negotiated the confusing traffic patterns out of the town. Once she had got clear, the traffic thinned and she glanced in the rear view mirror. *Ford Focus cars are very popular over here, she mused* – then remembered it was one of the cars commonly used by the rental agency and that it was the height of the holiday season, and a new week, with a new bunch of vacationers on their way to the shore. She hoped they would have a good time.

She was coming to the end of the section of the road that ran beside the estuary. The roundabout was just ahead and she veered off on the first exit when she caught sight of a sign pointing to the military airfield.

She did not know what she hoped to accomplish and had turned off on a whim. But she need not have worried – It followed the pattern of the rest of her day – she quickly came to a barrier across the road and the marine guard would not answer any questions, just telling her to "Please turn around and go back the way you came, this is military property."

She got the message and turned around, back to the roundabout, and back on the road to the village.

She was close to tears and suddenly very tired. She pulled off into a lay-by and sat there immobile for a long time, her mind gone totally blank. Finally, she came back to the present and sat there watching the passing vehicles until she felt together again, then put the car in gear and joined the traffic heading home for dinner.

She didn't want to go there, she had been resisting going there, but she knew it was inevitable that she would find herself back at the old pub opposite the church. She didn't want to go back to the hotel either so when she reached the center of the village she turned the steering wheel and negotiated the narrow streets back to the pub.

It was less crowded this time, it was still early evening and the few people there were obvious regulars, everyone joining in one conversation, bantering back and forth on a first name basis. She went up to the bar and ordered a scotch and was quickly included in their circle.

"You on holiday then?" One of them asked.

She acknowledged that she was, and then added that she'd visited the pub once before with a friend.

"You from America then?" Another asked after he'd heard her speak. And again she acknowledged she was.

The bartender broke in. "I remember your friend, he came back a couple of times after you'd had to go back to the States on business."

"How d'you know all that, John?" Someone called out from one of the tables.

"God, you must remember – it was the week that bugger who talked to everyone was here. He stood at my damn bar and talked my ear off – and anybody else's who happened to be around –wanted to know

everything about everyone, the nosy bastard. Not everyone liked it –
including your friend I seem to remember!" He said, turning to her.
The conversation splintered as everyone chimed in with their own
recollections and it gave her the chance to speak to just the bartender.
"Was the man still here when my friend came back?"
"Yes he was, he came up to get some beers while your friend was at the
bar and started talking to him again – that's how I know you were back
in the States last week. It was the same day the man met his two friends
– he said they were off to do some hiking around the coast. His friends
never talked at all, surly devils, but he talked enough for both of them
so you could understand it."
"This is a very weird question," she said casually, "but do you ever
remember them having toothpicks, maybe the toothpicks had colored
tops?"
She knew how her question sounded and the bartender's expression
mirrored her thoughts. He looked at her strangely for a second then
burst out laughing.
"Everyone in here has toothpicks if they eat the appetizers we put out
for happy hour – most of them have toothpicks stuck in them."
She wanted to press him about colored tops but before she could get up
the courage to go there, he changed the subject.
"Is your friend back in the States now?"
"My friend died last week."
"Oh my God, I am so sorry, I didn't know, was he the person who kil-?"
She broke in "He did not kill himself! I don't really think he slipped and
fell either, I don't know what happened. I wish I did."
They both went silent.
The door opened and a man and woman came in.
Relieved the bartender said, "New week, new holiday makers, it takes
them a day or two to find us."
Then to the couple who had now reached the bar. "What can I get you
folks?"
She put her empty glass down, thanked the bartender and said
goodbye. Several of the regulars waved to her as she left, and she
waved back. Outside she saw that the vacationing couple were driving a
blue Ford Focus and out of habit noted the license number.

She drove slowly back to the hotel, imagining the talk back in the pub "That was the woman-friend of the man who killed himself last week." *She knew that was what they thought...* She felt sick.

She parked the car. *Too tired tonight, search it tomorrow she told herself,* locked it, and climbed slowly up the hill and into the hotel. She was not used to moving so slowly – or thinking so slowly, she had no energy. She figured she must need food and went up to her room to wash up before going down to the dining room. It was an effort not to lie down on the bed and just close her eyes, but she forced herself to wash her face and comb her hair and go down to eat.

It was a different waiter who brought her the menu and in answer to his question, she said she would like a glass of red wine – the house wine would do. Nothing on the menu whetted her appetite, but she was only eating to keep going and would not enjoy any meal, however tasty it might be. She selected the smallest steak on the menu, ordered it rare and managed to eat half of it.

Back up in her room again she tried to plan what to do next, what she should do tomorrow – but she didn't want to think right then. She was tired and lonely and just wanted to get everything over with and get back to the States among her friends, and where she could talk with authorities who would help her and find out what had really happened. She decided to think about it tomorrow, after she had slept...

EIGHT

Staring at the ceiling early next morning she knew that the first thing she must do was to go to where he had died. That was the only connection to him that she had left and she dreaded going here, it was so final.

At breakfast next morning her usual waiter, as he did at all his tables, greeted her like an old friend and asked how she had enjoyed yesterday and asked what she had planned for today. She ignored his inquiries about her yesterday but shared that she was going to the Point today. A look of concern crossed his face as he remembered that was where her partner had died, and realized why she was going there.

"Please be careful." He said, "Are you going alone, is there anyone you can take with you?"

"I need to go by myself." She replied, "And I will be careful, but I need to see where it happened."

The waiter realized she was having a hard time with the conversation and went on to his next table.

He returned in a little while with her breakfast.

"If you change your mind and want someone with you, I get off at twelve and could come with you. I would stay back so you could be by yourself but I would be there if you needed anything."

She thanked him for his thoughtfulness but turned down his offer.

So right after breakfast she set off alone for the Point.

She got in the car and headed north along the coast road ignoring the magnificent view of the Atlantic and not stopping in any of the scenic lay-bys off the side of the road. She could see the Point in the distance jutting far out into the ocean beyond another wide stretch of sand. She thought about him almost exactly one week ago hiking along the cliff, crossing the sandy bay and having lunch in a pub before going on to the Point. Hers was a very different trip. This was something she needed to do for him – as well as for her, and she was not out to admire the scenery.

The road took a hairpin turn then dropped steeply down to the next bay. She had to stop at the bottom of the hill as a flock of holiday-makers carrying all their gear crossed the road from the carpark and wound their way down a narrow path, then down a flight of steps, then over rocks, to the beginning of the sand.

She started the car up again and continued along the increasingly narrow road towards the far end of the bay. Holiday chalets dotted each side of the road behind tall hedges. A huge double decker bus came towards her at a fast lick and she drove into the hedge as far as possible to avoid it – hoping it wouldn't scratch the side of the car and that the side mirror would stay in place. The bus didn't slow down as it passed and she continued around the blind corners more cautiously. A short while later she came to a picturesque cluster of old buildings – a small village consisting mainly of ice cream shops, "Ye Olde Teashops," a couple of pubs and a post office. Here the road ended. To the right a road branched off following a stream inland, a signpost pointing to more small villages hidden among the hills and to the route back to the coast north of the village. To the left, a road went to the far end of the bay, and then continued on, dead ending at the Point.

She turned to the left. The road was a little wider now and the holiday chalets were replaced by larger homes – guest houses and bed and breakfasts. A mile further on she came to the turnaround for the buses, complete with a bench and bus shelter and a wide path leading down to the far end of bay. Past the turnaround the road led to the Point. The road got narrower and more twisting, and tall stone walls replaced the earlier tall hedges, and behind the walls on the cliff-side, magnificent large homes faced the sea.

At the end of the road she turned into the National Trust Carpark. A few cars had got there before her and she turned her car around and backed

65

into a parking space close to the exit where she would not get blocked in if the carpark got busy. She paid the fee, locked the car, and started out to walk to the end of the Point.

The first part of the trail was wide and dusty and not very interesting. She looked back after she had been walking for a while and saw that several more cars were now in the carpark. Another car pulled up as she watched – another Ford Focus she mused – then an unwelcome thought came to her, another *blue* Ford Focus, and she watched as a man and a woman got out. From where she stood she couldn't tell if it was the same couple in the same car as the people who had showed up at the pub, but if it was... Where they following her? How could they have known that she would there? *Was she being paranoid? Christ, get over it, let it go!* But all the same, she did not want to be way out on the Point on the edge of the cliffs with them coming up behind her. She was beginning to wish she had taken the waiter up on his offer to come with her.

She was about to pass the walled garden – open to the public for a fee. She hadn't planned to stop there, but now she paid the admission and went in – that way she would get a better look at the couple as they passed. A family was already there, the woman taking her time admiring the flowers while the man and their two boys champed at the bit wanting to get on to the Point. She started to talk to the woman about the beautiful flowers, planning to attach herself to the family when they left the garden. And she was glad she did because when the man and woman appeared at the entrance she recognized them at once – it was the couple who had come into the pub the night before. *It's just a coincidence she told herself...* But even if it was, she was scared.

She left the safety of the walled garden with the family and started along the narrowing cliff path to the Point. It had become a given that she would join them and the woman was grateful to have someone to talk to. The boys rushed ahead, their father keeping pace with them, corralling them away from the edge of the cliffs.

By now she and the woman were walking single file, the woman ahead, talking over her shoulder. The waves crashing on the rocks below muffled their words, discouraging conversation, and pretty soon they were walking in silence. For that she was grateful. She had not shared why she was there and did not intend to, she dreaded going to where he had died and had no idea what she would feel – or what her reaction would be when she got there, her stomach was tied in knots. She let the sound of the waves fill her head.

Eventually they came to where the Coastal Path looped around and found the man and the two boys waiting for them to join them on the last steep and difficult trail to the end.

"Come on Mom!" One of the boys called.

"No fear!" His mother replied, "I'll wait for you here. Be careful."

Then turning to her she said, "Are you going to try it?"

"I think I will." She said carefully, trying to keep any emotion out of her voice.

She and the man and the two boys negotiated the trail slowly, avoiding the gaps in the path and staying close to each other, the man going first choosing their route with her bringing up the rear, the two boys sandwiched between them. Finally the trail – and the land – ended, and they were on a flat grassy plateau with only a vast ocean in front of them. A rope cordoned off the very edge of the cliff with a sign forbidding anyone to cross, warning of unstable ground. They did as they were told, the man placing a firm hand on the shoulders of his two sons to reinforce the message. The views were majestic and not limited by the rope. The boys were awe-struck.

She was left to herself staring down at the rocks below. A feeling of horror, sadness, fear and loss welled up inside her and she felt physically sick. It was so incredibly far down and so *final*. She wondered if he knew he was going to die, was he scared? Did he have time to think? Or did he only see the jagged rocks and knew he could not avoid them... She wondered if he had thought the surf would cushion his fall. She tried not to cry, she did not want to be asked why she was upset – and made a silent promise to him that she would find out the truth. She did not want the vision of him dead on the jagged rocks to be the last picture in her head. *But how could she avoid it...* Somehow the surf was comforting, softening the image. She hoped the waves had soothed his body and his spirit. *This was not how she had imagined it. This was not how she thought she would feel.*

She backed away from the edge unable to stay there any longer, trying not to throw up, wishing there was somewhere she could sit down, longing for him to be there with her and that none of this had ever happened, trying not to think of him dead on the rocks.

"Are you all right?" The man had seen her reaction.

"Yes, just a little vertigo," she lied.

Why can't I tell the truth? Why do I have to keep it a secret? This family would be genuinely supportive. But then she answered her own questions – ever since she arrived she had tried to make people listen to what had really happened and no one had believed her – and she knew this family would be no different – just peg her as depressed – and paranoid if she told them he was killed. She had looked carefully at the edge of the cliff – there was no sign of recent rock falls, or of the cliff having broken away, no scuff marks, no pieces of turf missing, nothing. She hadn't known what to expect, how she would feel. How *should* she feel? In her mind she had imagined she would be there by herself and would feel connected to him and be able to get some feeling of closure. *And letting go... Maybe this was what people called closure? But it hadn't helped... It raised more feelings, more acute feelings of loss... What had she expected?* All she wanted to do now was to go back up the trail. Seeing where he had died had not helped. It hadn't given her closure, and now she could not get the vision of him smashed on the rocks out of her head... *Would it have been any different if she had been there by herself? What might she have done if she had been alone?* Suddenly she was glad the family was there with her.

She looked up to where the woman was standing on the main path. She was talking to the couple from the blue Ford Focus... *Shit! They were the only reason she was not by herself, what should she do now?* Suddenly she was angry. The man gathered the boys to go back up the trail and she joined them. He paused to take a photo of his wife and she saw the couple quickly say their goodbyes and turn to continue along the main path. *They didn't want me to meet them, any more than I wanted them to meet me, she thought – or maybe they didn't want their photo taken...*

She and her new found friends walked together back the way they had come. It took them the best part of an hour and she joined the wife in sporadic conversation. Her sudden anger had faded away and she found talking kept her thoughts at bay. Jumbled thoughts, mixed thoughts, no thoughts – she couldn't sort through them. With every step she felt energy leaving her body and by the time they reached the carpark she was drained. Physically and mentally she was at a low ebb.

They said their goodbyes thanking each other for the company, and exchanged emails so the husband could send her copies of the photos he had taken. The two boys were clamoring for food but she turned down their offer to join them for a meal, pleading tiredness.

"You do look a bit tired." The woman said. "Are you all right? Some food might do you good."

She assured them that she was fine and they got in their car and left, the boys waving until they were out of sight. She waved back then turned to go to her car and breathed a sigh of relief when she realized the blue Ford Focus had already left.

What now? What was left to do? She got in the car and started driving slowly back to the hotel, tired and depressed without a clue what she should do next. At the crest of the cliff road she pulled into one of the lay-bys overlooking the ocean. The sun was low in the sky. It shone in her eyes and rippled over the waves below her. She sat there watching it gradually sink below the horizon turning the sea and sky around it red, then orange then yellow, and then the sea turned indigo and it was dusk.

A car pulled up behind her with its lights on and she realized it was almost dark and she should move on. She started the car, turned on her own headlights and her indicator and leaned out of the window to make sure the road was clear before she pulled out – and saw that the car that had just pulled in was a blue Ford Focus. She was just able to make out the color, but the light was not good enough to read the license plate or to see who was in the car.... but then the car door opened and a man started to get out.... She put her car in gear and screeched out of the lay-by. The hotel was about a minute away and she pulled up to the front entrance and gave the keys to the doorman. Let them park it tonight, she thought.

Once she was safely back in the hotel and had stopped shaking she had time to think. *Another coincidence? Lots of blue Fords on the road, the man could have just wanted to get a better look at the view.* She would never know, but she didn't think so and it unnerved her. She went straight to the dining room; she knew she should probably have tidied up first but she needed to be where there were other people – she was afraid to be alone. The dinner waiter came over and she ordered a scotch while she looked at the menu. He looked at her with what appeared to her to be concern, and she figured she must really look like hell. She hoped the scotch would restore her social face.

Dinner and two glasses of wine helped, and by the time she had finished eating she had made a decision. She had to get out of there – there was no reason to stay any longer…. She was scared and lonely and depressed – and she was not used to being patronized, not listened to, not believed – and she hated their pity. It was useless trying to get anything accomplished on this side of the Atlantic. She needed to get home to the States where she knew how to go about getting an investigation started, and where people knew her. Briefly she toyed with the idea of going up to London to talk to someone at the American Embassy, but no she decided, that would be just as futile, just another bureaucracy, another delay.

She went up to the room and started packing. She had hardly unpacked anything, so she tackled his things first, searching again for the list of text numbers and anything else to help to prove what had happened. She hoped he had left everything back in his apartment and it wasn't one of the things the phony husband had taken. She had never found his passport and was pretty sure that was gone. The packing did not take long – he had one suitcase and his brief bag and by squeezing some of his clothes into her carryon she managed to get the briefcase in the suitcase. Not bad she thought, just two cases. What next? Tomorrow she would empty out the car. Tonight she had to try to change her reservation. Originally they had planned to go back on Sunday, he to New York, she to Philadelphia, but now she wanted to bring her flight forward and go to New York so she could check his apartment – maybe she would find some proof there. With that in mind she got her ticket changed to Thursday evening, leaving from Heathrow and going into Kennedy instead of Philadelphia.

Once she had done that, she sat down at the desk in her room, pulled out some of the hotel writing paper, and wrote a detailed account of everything that had happened in the last three months. She wrote in long hand – the first time she had done that for a long time but she wanted to mail copies back to the States – both to herself at her Philadelphia address, and to her best friend at work. Maybe she was being paranoid but she felt the need for someone other than herself to know what had been going on for the last few months. *If no one would listen, maybe they would read what she had been trying to tell them.* Then she typed a synopsis into her phone, and saved it to the cloud – but somehow she was getting more and more concerned that her phone had been hacked.... She grabbed a couple of envelopes, planning to go into the village first thing in the morning, first to make copies at the local library and then to mail them direct from the post office – she did not trust leaving them with the outgoing mail at the hotel, too many things could go wrong.... She glanced at the bedside clock and saw that it was already Wednesday morning.

NINE

She woke up four hours later and a little after nine went to the bell captain and asked him to have the parking attendant bring her car round. It was only two miles to the village and she found a carpark right outside the library. She paid at the machine and displayed the ticket on her car's dashboard as instructed, then walked over to the library – only to find it would not open for another thirty minutes. Luckily there was a cafe on the other side of the carpark and she went in and ordered a coffee. She was sitting there drinking her coffee when she saw a blue Ford Focus go slowly by, a man driving with a woman beside him... *Was it them? How the hell could they know where she would be! It was almost as if they were trac...* then it sunk in, she needed to check her car for a tracking device.

If that *was* the couple they knew where she was – and she did not want them to know what she was doing. She asked the woman behind the counter if there was anywhere other than the library where she could get copies made and the woman directed her to the post office.

"The post office does a lot more than stamps and letters, Dear. You can make your copies and buying picture postcards too, if you like."

Thank God! She didn't have to wait for the library to open. She paid her bill and left quickly, cutting through the alley to the main street and the post office. Ten minutes later her notes were copied and safely mailed and she felt almost relaxed. She left the post office carefully, making sure that she was not seen, and spent the next half hour in the village, acting like a true holiday maker – buying a newspaper, some fruit, and some postcards – staying with other tourists and not caring if they saw her or not.

Back at the hotel she parked the car for herself in the guest carpark, and searched the inside carefully in case he had hidden anything there, and then the outside for a tracking device. The inside revealed nothing new. Outside it was a different story. A short search and she found a tracking device attached under the front bumper. She made sure that there wasn't a second one anywhere but left the one she had found where I was – for now – so no one would know she had found it. She picked up his windbreaker and put the rental agreement and the book on North Devon in the plastic bag with the fruit and postcards, and climbed up the path to the hotel, thinking all the time about what to do next. Should she report the tracking device? She no longer trusted anyone. By now she had become convinced that no one would listen to her. If she went to the police with the same story again she could hear them explain to her that some rental companies put devices on their cars. *She could hear them say it. Why waste the time... Was she being paranoid?...*

She knew she could not stay the last night in the hotel now that she had found the device, but she didn't want anyone to know that she had left either. *Was there anything she had forgotten to do before she took off?* She had to make sure she had left no stone left unturned that would prove what had really happened. In one of his last texts he had said he was trying to put his thoughts down to clear his head, and she had hoped that like her, he had written something on paper. It occurred to her that he might have used the hotel safe, so before she returned to her room she went to the front desk, gave the room number and both their names and asked if they were keeping anything for them in the safe. But no they weren't – another dead end.

She was frustrated and depressed, so many dead ends. If he had written anything on paper she realized it would have been one of the first things the phony "brother-in-law" would have taken when he had searched the room. His blackberry was gone, his laptop was gone – and his mobile was either at the bottom of the ocean or had also been taken by the "brother-in-law". The information it held was probably still floating around in the Cloud somewhere, but she did not know his passwords – one more reason for her to go to his apartment where she might be able to find something to help her figure them out.

It was just gone eleven, she had to get going... Once in the room she squashed his windbreaker, and for some reason the book on North Devon, into his case and closed it up. She left the room wheeling it behind her and took the back elevator down, pressing the lowest button and getting out on the ground floor to go out to the patio. From there she could get to the carpark without going through the lobby. It took only a few seconds to put his case safely in the trunk and she retraced her steps across the patio and into the hotel. She was pretty sure no one had noticed her. *Half way there she thought....*

The manager caught up with her as she was walking through the lounge on her way back. She hadn't realized he was behind her.

"How are you doing?" He asked. "Are you going to stay until Saturday?"

"Yes, I think I will," she lied, then added. "If anyone asks, please don't say I'm here, and can you please make sure that your staff doesn't tell anyone either, I don't want anyone to know where I am."

"Of course. No one will know you are here, and I'll make sure that the staff preserves your privacy too. Does that include his sister if she tries to contact you?"

"She and her husband more than anyone! She was a phony – my partner did not have a sister – or a brother for that matter, I don't know who they were but they damn well weren't his sister and brother-in-law, and I have been trying to find out what all this means and what really happened ever since you told me... but no one believes me, and I can see that you don't either." She was close to tears. "It doesn't matter – I've given up trying to get anyone to listen."

She broke away but he caught up with her again.

"But they showed me proof – driver licenses, credit cards..."

"All false!" she replied. "Look you have been very nice to me and I don't blame you, but they took you in."

"Why didn't you tell me this when I told me about his death? I know the coroner checked them out too, have you talked to him?" Now he was upset.

74

"Oh yes, I talked to the coroner, I told him the whole story – he was very nice, and very patronizing and very dis-believing. He gave me lip service."

She paused, "And why didn't I tell you when you told me he was dead? I couldn't think straight, I was trying to come to grips with what you had just told me and everything else you said didn't register until it was past. – All I could think was my partner was dead. Many strange things have happened the last three months and when you said his *sister* had taken his body and I knew he didn't *have* a sister, I couldn't handle it, I closed down. I guess I needed time to sort it out. But yes, I did tell the Coroner the whole story, not that he listened..."

She literally fled from him, leaving him standing there looking after her with a worried expression on his face.

As soon as she got back to the room she threw the last remaining things in her carryon. She paused as she was about to pack her toothbrush and toothpaste and decided to leave them to reinforce the lie that she was still there, she could always buy new ones. The room had already been made up so she ran the shower for a minute and wet several towels so they looked used and then went to the bed and unmade it. Back to the bathroom she brushed her teeth again – one last time she thought. A quick final look around the room then she swung her bag onto her shoulder, grabbed the "Do not Disturb" sign and hung it on the door, and left wheeling her carryon.

Down the back elevator, across the patio, down to the carpark for the second time that morning, and she got to the car without incident. She was pretty sure she had not been seen. There was one last thing she had to do. She went to the front of the car and carefully pulled the tracking device off the bumper. Her car was parked in the first row, facing out with a view of the beach. A solid metal railing prevented guests driving off the edge of the cliff and now she 'relocated' the device on the far side of the post directly in front of her car. Then she disabled the Google and GPS apps in her mobile – just in case.

She drove north along the coast, back towards the small village on the way to the Point, but this time in the center where the road divided, she turned right instead of left, and drove on carefully through tortuously narrow and twisting lanes and small coastal villages before finally turning inland and up onto the beginning of the downs. It was slower, but she knew from the last few days that GPS and Wi-Fi were very limited in the more remote areas.

The landscape changed abruptly when she reached the open rolling moors and the driving became easier though lonelier, very few cars shared the road with her. At first she could see for miles, but then the weather closed in, obliterating the moors, curtains of rain sheeting across the road. Her windshield wipers going full blast could not keep up with the deluge.

Gradually the rain let up and she drove on slowly for several hours avoiding main roads wherever possible and watching the scenery change – becoming more civilized, tamed, more built up. Lanes turned into country roads and she stopped for a late lunch in one of the many small towns. It was close to Bath and she thought maybe she would stay there for the night, it would be easy to get onto the motorways in the morning – and it was only about ninety miles to London from there. In normal times she would have enjoyed visiting the historic Georgian town with its' Roman Baths, but today it didn't even cross her mind.

In the end she finished up staying just south of Bath in an attractive old farmhouse in a room up under the eaves.

Thursday morning she drove to London, blending into the heavy traffic on the motorways, and made good time, getting to the rental car return around noon. The rental agency was about twenty minutes from Heathrow and she had plenty of time before her flight to take the shuttle to her terminal.

She pulled into the express line so she could return the car without going into the office, grabbed a luggage cart, loaded both of their bags on it, and waited for the man with the clipboard to check her in. So it was a complete surprise when he took one look at her license plate and rental agreement and told her she would need to go into the office to complete the paperwork. Both their names were on the rental agreement so she could not see why she had been singled out, but she got the strong impression that arguing would get her nowhere. She followed him into the office, pushing the cart with the suitcases in front of her and was led, not to the counter but to a small private office in the back. A man in his forties wearing the agency uniform approached her, smiled and shook her hand. Without preamble he started to speak. "This is something that we have never had happen before. About two weeks ago we got an envelope in the mail and when we opened it there was another, sealed envelope inside with your rental agreement number and the license number of the car you rented. Oh – and there was also a brief note asking us to give it to you when you returned the car." He handed her the envelope and added "As you can see, it's also marked personal, and we have not opened it."

She was floored. "I have no idea what this is or who might have sent it. Do you still have the envelope it came in, or the note?"

"I'm afraid not. Unfortunately, one of the evening staff threw it out thinking it was garbage, I'm sorry."

She asked if there had been a return address on their envelope and he said he did not remember one. She looked at the envelope carefully, holding it as if it was toxic, but did not open it. She dropped it into her bag, she needed to be alone before she did that....

The shuttle dropped her at the terminal and first thing she checked both bags. She glanced up at the departure board, plenty of time before she had to go through security, and found a restroom. But she didn't get the envelope out of her bag again until she was sitting on the commode with the door locked. Carefully, trying not to tear it, she pried the flap open and looked inside. No written note – only bank notes, one hundred dollar bills, fifty of them. *What the hell should she do with them?* She took the notes out of the envelope and put them in the two inside pockets of her shoulder bag. Then she put the car rental papers in the envelope and put that in her bag as well. She would figure out what to do with them when she got back to the States.

She got through the passport check and security without any problems and had plenty of time for an unrushed dinner in one of the restaurants on the far side. One more interminable wait at the gate after dinner and she was in her seat on the plane taxi-ing down the runway.

The plane lifted off, tipping her back in her seat as it went into a steep climb to clear the clouds. She breathed out. *Halfway home – and no sign of the couple in the blue Ford Focus since she left the hotel.*

She would have felt a lot more relaxed if it hadn't been for the envelope the rental agency had given her... she assumed it was for expenses for the weekend in Devon when they had stuck that first damn toothpick in the old doorframe. *God! She wished he hadn't agreed to do that – everything would have been so different.* She still could not believe he was dead and almost expected to find him back in his apartment. *After all, she had absolutely no proof he was dead – jut hearsay from a group of people she didn't know and who she didn't trust. Maybe they were all part of this? What else would he have told her this week if he had hadn't been killed? She knew he had been killed...* The energy flooded out of her body leaving panic behind. *He was gone, she would never see him again – ever. Who could she confide in now? She was alone.* They were flying into the night and it was dark outside the plane. It only emphasized the void she was feeling... She closed her eyes and tried to sleep, but it was no good – too many jumbled thoughts running through her brain. *Who should she contact to investigate what had happened? .... Would they believe her any more than the people in England? There was no proof of anything – except perhaps the envelope of money, but there was nothing that would tie that to his death – She must go to his apartment first thing .... She must try to find the text and phone numbers he had saved .... She must try to find his passwords too.... She must get all the information together and then take it to the FBI or someone.* It suddenly occurred to her that unknown people may have already been to his apartment and that part of the network was in the States as well as in England. They obviously were a lot more sophisticated than either of them had realized. Suddenly she didn't feel so safe anymore and panic rose to the surface again.

But she was so sad, and so weary, and so very, very tired. There was nothing more she could do – *she would just have to leave it to fate –*she finally drifted off to sleep.

She was woken up by people moving about the plane and the pilot coming on to let them know they would land in forty minutes, the weather was fine and local time was just after ten.

Soon the plane landed, and like lemmings all two hundred passengers rushed towards the baggage claim – and waited – again - until a motor started up, jerking the carousel to life and their bags started to spew out of the center chute and tumble down onto the carousel, spinning around until they were dragged off by thankful owners. She followed the others, first getting a luggage cart –wondering why she had to pay here in the States when they were free in most of Europe – and quickly retrieved her cases. She headed for the Customs and Immigration lines.

The Customs and Immigration Officer was sitting on a high chair behind a high desk, behind a thick glass panel. He took her US passport and ran it through the scanner on his desk.
"Anything to declare?" He asked, chewing his gum.
She wanted to say, *"Yes someone left me $5,000 in an envelope."* But she didn't. She shook her head, "No."
"What was the reason for your trip?"
She wanted to say, *"I went to join my partner but he had been killed."* But she didn't. "Vacation." She said.
"Welcome home," he said with a smile and handed her back her passport.
She wanted to say, *"I'm being followed."* But she didn't.
"Thank you." She said.

She walked on through the airport, out to taxi rank.
And it was no surprise and almost a relief when someone tapped her on the shoulder and offered her a ride. *Now they'll know I wasn't being paranoid, they'll have to believe me, she thought* as someone put a firm grip on her elbow and steered her to a car.
But please, will someone see that this is really happening?

The car glided away from the curb out into the stream of traffic leaving the airport.
Someone shouted "Hey! You forgot your bags …"

But the car had disappeared into the night.

THE STATES

TEN

The last weekend in July had come and gone. Monday promised to be another hot day. Commuter traffic already clogged the roads around Philadelphia, the cars weaving in and out of the lanes in a complicated pavane. The weekday ritual was under way.

On the outskirts of the city those employed at the headquarters of an international corporation joined the throng. Their work environment had been carefully crafted and they drove to an impressive building surrounded by park-like grounds. Once past the inevitable security desk, the foyer opened to a huge circular atrium five stories high, topped, appropriately, with a glass ceiling framing a view of the sky. On each floor, showcase walkways circled the walls with corridors like spokes of a wagon wheel leading off to hidden offices. A wide open spiral staircase soared upwards in the middle of the space – glass banisters installed for safety reasons – then floated down to the ground level which sported an upscale self-serve cafeteria. Off to one side a wall of glass opened to a secluded patio. For those unwilling to climb the stairs, elevators found hidden down the corridors whooshed to the upper floors. A modern building oozing healthy living.

Two women approached each other on the fourth floor walkway. As they passed, one asked the other, "Where's Jill?"

"I have no idea," the other replied irritably, "Is she due back today?"

"I thought so, but maybe she's still off with Jack somewhere…."

"Who's Jack?" The other asked.

"I was just making a joke, Jack, Jill, get it?" the first woman replied, "She's been on vacation with her friend in England, that's not his name – she keeps to herself, or they keep to themselves, they have an exclusive club of two."

"I haven't seen her today and I'm not sure when her vacation is over."

"Maybe I got it wrong and she's not back 'til next week."

They continued on their separate ways...

The woman who had opened the conversation was a friend of Jill's – really more a good acquaintance, sharing the occasional lunch and even more occasionally, dinner. Although they enjoyed each other's company, their friendship was based on their work and they rarely socialized outside its sphere. They worked in different departments – hence the inquiry to the woman she passed on the fourth floor who was in the same department as Jill. She pondered over their friendship as she entered the corridor leading to her office. She missed Jill's sense of humor and approach to life when she was not around, they shared many of the same interests and so would seek out each other's company when they were both in the building, but they travelled a lot which was another barrier to them getting to know each other better. What did she really know about her? Well, she knew her parents lived in New Jersey, in Princeton, and although Jill lived and worked only forty minutes away, she didn't see them very often. And she knew she had a very close friend named Ted who lived and worked in New York, and that she and Ted spent every weekend together – that's the main barrier, the woman thought – her friend was not likely to spend time on the singles circuit, as she herself did.

She reached her office and forgot about her musings as she approached the beginning of another hectic work week.

Princeton, New Jersey. A lazy time in the town, the fall semester would not start for another six weeks and only summer session students were in town. It made parking a little easier, and the sidewalks a little less crowded. The weather was hot but the town maintained its demeanor, proud of its lifestyle; its University; Einstein, and its heritage dating back to the battles of the Revolutionary War. It had managed to preserve its picturesque appearance over the years, with historic buildings and narrow tree-lined streets branching off the main thoroughfare and all in all was a very pleasant place to live. The townspeople boasted about their museums, their university, their upscale shops, their good restaurants and the train to New York City, but if only the parking were better they complained......

Down one of the tree-lined streets the phone rang and a woman answered it. On the other end a man from the security office at Kennedy Airport inquired if Jill Davis was there. The woman replied that she was not, then identified herself as her mother, and asked if she could help. The man went on to explain that Jill's two bags had been found outside an exit door near the taxi rank and that she must have taken a cab and forgotten her bags, could they deliver them to her. He explained that they had tried her home and work numbers, emails and cell phone with no success and that the Princeton number of her parents was the last contact on the list she had registered with the airline.

The two bags were delivered that afternoon. In the meantime, Jill's mother also tried to reach her, trying all of the numbers and emails she had, and then reaching out to the few friends she knew about, all without success. It did not worry her unduly – although she was surprised that her capable daughter had left her bags behind – that was totally unlike her, she thought. Even though Princeton was less than an hour's drive from Philadelphia, their daughter visited rarely. Her parents would have liked to see her more, but at this time in their lives their relationship was amicable, but not close. In earlier years Jill had been a free spirit, demanding her independence, and her parents had not understood, or supported many of the decisions she had made, they had worried about her future security and had breathed a sigh of relief when she finally focused on her career and started to climb the corporate ladder. Now the three of them had a pleasant "home for the holidays" kind of relationship. Absent of open conflicts but not sharing – or seeking – advice for day to day issues. They were in the comfortable middle period of life, when parents are still healthy and active, and offspring have settled into their own separate lives.

Back in Philadelphia a letter had been delivered to the friend's office on the fourth floor. She was surprised that Jill had bothered to write while she was on vacation, and even more surprised that she had resorted to snail mail. She opened the letter and her surprise turned to disbelief.

Moira – Ted is dead. He was found on the rocks at the bottom of some cliffs 3 days before I got here. Everyone thinks he killed himself. I'm sure he was killed. …. She read on with increasing concern. She too spent the next few hours trying to find Jill, with increased urgency but without success.

Finally, she tried to reach someone at the New York Company where Jill's friend Ted had worked. She had met Ted once, briefly, and had liked him. The three of them had passed a pleasant evening exchanging pleasantries and work horrors, so she knew a little about his work environment and the people he worked with. Jill's letter had told her that Ted was dead, but maybe his company had more information about what had happened, maybe they could shed light on where Jill might be – perhaps she was in New York... She called the main number and asked to speak to one Dan Murphy. His was the only name she remembered from their evening together and she could not remember if he was an associate or Ted's boss.

He answered the phone after two rings, "Dan Murphy."

She introduced herself.

"Hi, my name is Moira Gregory, you don't know me, but I work with Ted's friend Jill." She offered her condolences. "I was so sorry to learn about Ted's death, please accept my sympathy."

"What are you talking about?" Dan answered, "Ted and Jill are on vacation in England, he will be in the office tomorrow."

Suddenly she realized – *No one knows what has happened, God! –he's been dead for almost two weeks...* Quickly she tried to explain about the letter she had received that day from Jill, written while she was still in Devon, telling her that Ted was dead, and the murky circumstances surrounding his death, and the strange events that had occurred since then.

She went on to voice her concerns for Jill.

"I have been trying to reach her ever since I opened her letter, but she seems to have disappeared. I was hoping she had gone to New York."

While she was talking she realized that Dan was probably not taking in anything she was saying.

"Wait!" from Dan. "You're telling me that Ted is dead? Is this a joke? Because if it is, it's in very bad taste. Who are you?"

She started again from the beginning, first apologizing for bringing such terrible news. She had thought that Ted's company would have been notified of his death and had not realized that no one was aware of what had happened. She told him again about the very disturbing letter she had just received from Jill and that no one had believed Jill when she had gone to the authorities.

Dan interrupted "Can you scan her letter and send it to me?" He gave her his email.

"I'll call you back when I've read it, this makes no sense – Ted, is dead? That can't be right! There must be some mix-up. Christ, that's unbelievable!"

She was in the process of scanning the letter when the woman who she had talked with that morning appeared in the doorway.

"Got a minute Moira? I just got a very strange call from Jill's mother. Apparently Jill's bags were left near the taxi rank at JFK – the airlines delivered them to her because they couldn't reach Jill – her mother hasn't been able to reach her either, she's been trying all day."

The letter finished going through the scanner and she emailed it to Dan Murphy before she answered. Her first thought was to keep the letter to herself. She hesitated, but then picked it up and handed it to her co-worker.

"Read this, it showed up on my desk today."

In New York Dan started reading the letter as soon as it arrived in his email.

Moira – Ted is dead. He was found on the rocks at the bottom of some cliffs 3 days before I got here. Everyone thinks he killed himself. I'm sure he was killed. Weird things have been happening – I'm sure they're connected but no one believes me. I need someone outside of this god-forsaken place to know what has been going on. Please. This is serious and I'm scared – if anything happens and I don't get back home you need to know what happened. I'm writing this long-hand because I think my phone has been hacked. Please believe me, I know this sounds unreal. I've tried to write everything down in the correct order.

Back in February I saw an ad in a newspaper I'd found when Ted and I were in a diner, and joked to him that he should answer it. The ad was looking for someone who was going to be in the UK in July to "do them a favor" in return for a free weekend in Devon. I knew Ted was going to be there on business and he was always talking about Devon because he had vacationed there when he was a kid. It was a joke! I didn't know he'd continue the joke and had replied to the ad until much later. A man called him the following week and told him the 'favor' was nothing illegal and he would learn the details later. The only thing the man insisted on was secrecy. Ted waited to see what developed. Every couple of weeks he got texts with pieces of information. He couldn't trace the numbers. (He's left a list of them in his apartment). He got hooked, but started to worry about what he was getting into. That's when he told me. It was bizarre – He was to paint the tips of 5 flat toothpicks, one each blue, yellow, green, orange and red. By June he had been given directions to a parish church in a village 2 miles from the North Devon Coast. He was to go to the original gatehouse entrance and wedge one of the toothpicks in a crack in the doorframe of the old door he would find on the right-hand wall of the passageway into the churchyard. We decided that I would go too for the weekend. I'd fly back on Monday and he would go on to his meetings.

Sat- 7/5. We arrived in the UK and stayed at an old inn on Exmoor that night and Sunday.

(All addresses – where we stayed; toothpicks locations; police station; church; pubs; crematorium; hotel on the coast etc. on a separate sheet at end of letter).

Sun- 7/6. a.m. Ted wedged the blue-tipped toothpick into a crack of the doorframe of the gatehouse door (no one saw him) then joined me at the beach. Glorious day and we decided to come back for a vacation after his meetings. I couldn't make it until the 19th so Ted would be there for a week by himself before I flew back. Ted made reservations at the hotel overlooking the beach where we had gone for a drink. On the way back to the inn we went to check on the toothpick and found it had gone!! There is an old pub opposite the gatehouse and we went in for a drink. Ted went to get our drinks and at the bar there was an overly friendly man talking to everyone – but the really unnerving thing was he was picking his teeth with the blue-tipped toothpick!! We figured that he was trying to contact someone who would recognize its significance. (Ted did not let on that he had put it the doorframe).

Late Sun p.m. back at the inn, Ted got a text requesting he place 2 more toothpicks before the following Sunday – 1 in an old lighthouse chapel in a town 8 miles N.E of the first toothpick, and the other in an old chantry chapel in the market town 8 miles S.E of the first one. I did not want him to do any more, but he was determined, he always followed things through to the end.

Mon- 7/7. I went back to Philly. Ted stayed and had meetings all week.

The following is what he wrote me after he got back to Devon

Fri-7/11. He drove across the moors to North Devon. On the way he placed the yellow tipped toothpick in the chapel in the town about 8 miles north of his hotel.

Sat-7/12 a.m. He ran 3 miles along the sand to the estuary and up into the dunes. He saw 2 "bird-watchers" with binoculars near the military compound. Sat. p.m. he drove to the market town and placed the green tipped toothpick in the flagstone step in front of the crypt entrance of the chantry. He also pushed the orange tipped one into a crack, he had been told to do that if he thought someone saw him – there was a couple putting flowers on a grave close by. (He thought they might have been the same couple who were at the lighthouse chapel the day before.)

Sun Evening- 7/13. He went back to the pub across from the church and was accosted by the man who had been picking his teeth with the blue tipped toothpick the previous Sunday. The man said he was meeting 2 friends, they were staying at the George Hotel and were going to hike the Heritage Trail. Without thinking Ted told him where he was staying when the man asked him. On the way out he passed their table and saw the paint-tipped toothpicks on their table – each one broken into 2 pieces. The men were watching him when he left the pub. Mon- 7/14 a.m. Ted saw the 3 men from the pub come into his hotel, look around the foyer and then they walked out again. Later the same day he ran along the sand turning up into the dunes near the military compound. He looked down at the estuary below and saw the same 3 men approaching along the estuary from the direction of the village. One of them climbed up into a beached cabin cruiser and lugged a long object out from the cabin and heaved it up over the side of the boat to the other two men who hid it close by in the ruins of an old light house. Ted though it looked like a rocket launcher. Then the men headed back over the Burrows towards the village.

Before dinner Ted went for a drink in the hotel bar and bumped into the same 3 men in the bar. The talkative one asked him if he had run along the sands <u>again</u>. Ted got the definite feeling that they had been watching him.

Tues- 7/15. Ted told me he had made detailed notes about what had been happening. He felt involved because he had placed those damn toothpicks which he knew were all part of it. Tues p.m. he took a trip to the other side of the estuary, on his way back he stopped at a police station in the market town and reported the 3 men taking something that looked like a rocket launcher off the boat in the estuary and hide it in the lighthouse ruins. (He didn't get the feeling the policeman would follow up on it). He wrote that the next day (Wednesday) he was going to hike to the Point.

That was the last text I got from him. (I never found the notes he had written, or his cell phone, tho' I turned our hotel room upside down after I got back here).

Sat (7/19) I flew back to the UK and took the train down.... At this point Dan paused, trying to take in what he had just read. He picked up the phone to call Moira...

The woman from Jill's department was still in Moira's office. Both women were now very concerned, they knew Jill tended to be a free spirit, but they also knew that she was unlikely to go off the grid when she was due back at work. She took her responsibilities seriously. They hoped that she was just being melodramatic in the letter, but the fact that no one had been able to contact her made them anxious. This was getting serious.

The phone rang and the woman started to leave, first handing Moira a piece of paper.

"Here's her mother's number, you know Jill better than I do, maybe you should call her. She should know about the letter."

"Thanks," Moira replied as she picked up the phone, "I'm going to. Let me know if you hear anything and I'll do the same."

The call was from Dan Murphy. He had read the first half of the letter and was beginning to come to grips with the fact that Ted was dead.

"I had to call you back, I haven't finished reading the letter yet – but I know Ted very well, he is a good friend, I still can't believe he's dead, but I know he wouldn't kill himself! I also think it's unlikely that he fell. He was not reckless and would not have gone near the edge of the cliff without making sure it was safe. Do you think Jill is being over dramatic? She can be you know…"

It had sunk in that this was not a joke, Ted was dead and Jill, for the moment could not be found. He knew he needed to read the rest of the letter to find out what had happened after Jill got back in England – but more urgent was the need to let Jill's friend know that Ted was not the kind of man who would ever kill himself.

"He doesn't sound like the type to jump off a cliff, and I don't think it was an accident," Moira replied. "You need to read the rest of Jill's letter. I'm really worried about her."

She realized that he was still trying to come to grips with Ted's death, while her total focus was now on her concern for Jill. *Where was she? …* She filled him in about the call from Jill's mother.

"I'm going to call her parents," she said. "I'm dreading it but they need to know what's going on, I'll drive over there this evening if they want to see me."

"Good." He said. "I need to finish the letter, but then I'm contacting my boss. I hope I can reach him, I think he's on some trade mission somewhere – and I'm about to go to HR to let them know. I know Ted didn't have any close family, but I think there may be an uncle somewhere, someone needs to let him know."

They agreed to keep in touch.

She put the phone down and sat at her desk without moving for a while. What was she going to say to Jill's parents? She re-read the second half of the Jill's letter

Sat- 7/19. I flew back to the UK and took the train down to North Devon .... Ted was supposed to meet me but he wasn't there. I had been trying to contact him since Wed, 7/16. I took a taxi to the hotel. When I got there they told me he was dead. It was awful. I couldn't believe it. I thought it was some horrible joke. ... The manager said his 'sister and brother-in-law' showed up on Thursday and took charge of everything. .... TED DID NOT HAVE A SISTER – OR A BROTHER.!! .... The 'brother-in-law' .... took Ted's passport and blackberry ... and God knows what else. ... they went to the coroner and got his body released, and then had him cremated. All in 2 days. ... It's all so horrible – there is nothing of Ted left, they vaporized him totally. That night I went down onto the sands and walked for hours trying to get my head together .... I saw a man standing in the shadows of the dunes .... I think he was watching me. ...

Monday (7/21) The far end of the beach was closed for Military exercises. I went to the market town 8 miles away (I found our rental car in the guest parking lot, the keys were in the refrigerator – Ted had hidden them).

I visited the police station, Coroner, and crematorium. Also tried to talk to someone at the military camp but could not get past the sentry.

-The police station. They did forward Ted's information to the village police-force and the military.

-Coroner, patronizing bastard. Totally taken in by the phony 'sister and brother-in-law'. I told him everything –but he didn't listen. Very defensive! I showed him the texts from Ted but he said that I hadn't seen any of the events in person – figured it was just Ted trying to get me to come over. Total balls.

-The woman at the crematorium was a total bitch. Ted's ashes were picked up by the phony couple on Friday. What did they do with him?

On the way back I went to the pub by the church ...As I was leaving a couple came in, I think they were following me. They were driving a blue Ford Focus, the same make/ color as the car behind me all the way from the market town. (I memorized the License plate# LF15MEO.) Everyone thinks Ted killed himself. I know he didn't.

Tues (7/22). I drove to the Point because I had to see where Ted died. Just after I got there a blue Ford Focus entered the parking lot and the same couple got out. I attached myself to a family I met on the Coastal Path.... I went down the last difficult part of the trail to the edge of the Point. Parts of the cliffs were undermined but where Ted was supposed to have gone over the edge it was <u>not</u> undermined. I am sure the 3 men had followed him and pushed him over. He couldn't have got passed them back up onto the Coastal Path. On the way back to the hotel I stopped in a layby off the cliff road. It was getting dark – a blue ford focus pulled in behind me and a man started to get out. I left fast.

-I have to get back home as soon as possible. .... I'm going to mail this from the village P.O tomorrow (Wed. 7/23) then leave ....

-I have changed my ticket to go to NYC on Thursday instead of Philly on Sunday. I'm going to check Ted's apartment for the phone list. ...

I'm not crazy Moira, if I don't make it back please get this to someone who can find out what really happened.

Please tell my parents I love them.

Jill

Finally Moira stood up and closed her door. She picked up her cell phone.

It rang once before a man answered. She identified herself as Jill's friend from work. He broke in before she had finished and she realized she was talking to her father.

"Any news? Have you managed to reach her?"

She had to admit she hadn't. *Now the difficult part she thought, how to tell them about the letter...*

"But I did get a letter from her today. I think you should read it. Her friend Ted died just before she got to Devon, she was told he had fallen over a cliff but she doesn't believe that's what happened. It all very

involved, and very disconcerting. The letter is long and frankly unnerving."

She asked if she could email it to them, or if it was easier for them, she
would drive to Princeton and give it to them in person. She could sense
the relief in his voice at her offer, answering how much Jill's mother and
he would appreciate it. She told him she could be there in about an
hour.

She packed up her work and let the office know she was leaving.

ELEVEN

Rumors were travelling fast – thanks to the corporate grapevine and the woman from Jill's department – and several people called out good luck as she left. *It's not me that needs the luck, its Jill, she thought – God! I hope she's all right.*
She had no hope of avoiding the traffic at that time of the day, but until she got close to Princeton she made good time. The address Jill's father had given her was close to the center of Princeton and the traffic turned into stop and crawl for the last few miles. At last she turned onto Nassau Street and several blocks down her GPS instructed her to turn left. Several more turns and she came to the street where Jill's parents lived. She was in a neighborhood of homes built in the 1920's. Jill's parents' home was no exception – a red brick house with a short driveway and steps up from the drive to the path to the front door. Jill's father had told her to park in the driveway in front of the garage – *Thank God, he'd suggested that* .... Cars were crowded in head to toe all along the narrow tree-lined street.

They had heard her arrive and by the time she had climbed the steps the front door was open. A man stood in the doorway. She figured he was probably in his early sixties, fairly tall, trim and starting to grey – she found herself wondering what his exercise regime was and if he worked at it. A woman appeared behind him. Very obviously she was upset, but Moira figured under normal circumstances they would both appear as confident and assured people. They complemented each other well. She too was tall – thinner than the man, with well-groomed blond hair cropped at chin length. *Into yoga and Pilates, Moira thought.* They pulled her into the house and ushered her into the living room. Cheese and crackers had been set out before she arrived and they offered her something to drink. She accepted a glass of water but passed on the food, she needed to get this over with…

Before she left her office Moira had made copies of Jill's letter and now she handed one to each of them. The woman sank into a chair to read, handling the letter as if it was fragile and starting to panic as she read, her eyes searching out her husband for support, but he remained standing, oblivious that she was looking for him. He scanned the letter quickly from start to finish then sat down abruptly and read it again, slowly from the beginning, studying each sentence carefully. At last he finished reading and searched out his wife. They both rose and met in the middle of the room, putting their arms around each other. They were shell shocked and had forgotten Moira was in the room. She wasn't sure what she should do. Should she bow out and make her exit? *Just leave… Slide out of the room before they noticed she had gone…* She desperately wanted to get away and leave them alone to comfort each other and to come to grips with what they had just read.

As if sensing her thoughts, Jill's mother broke away from her husband wiping her tears away from her eyes with both hands.

"Moira, please forgive us, you were so good to come all this way to bring us Jill's letter. We have to think what to do."

Her husband looked up, pulling himself together, visibly straightening his shoulders.

"Joan's right, we are being incredibly rude, and you have been so kind, and Jill's your friend, this must be hard for you too. Please stay, I think we all need a drink. What will you have?"

She marveled at their ability to regain their composure so quickly in front of an outsider. *Typical of their generation, still maintaining vestiges of their stiff upper lip formal background….* She wished she could be as strong. She accepted the vodka tonic he handed her.

He poured a second glass which he handed it to his wife.

"Joan, I'm going to call the police, we need their help to find Jill."

He left the room to make the call and his wife brought up the subject of the two suitcases that had been delivered earlier that day,

"They weren't locked. One of them is Ted's case. It has all of his work papers from the business meetings he had in England."

Moira realized where she was going.

"Would you like me to take it and give it to his boss Dan Murphy? I'm going to be talking to him later and I'm sure I can get it to him."

She was obviously relieved.

"Would you? That would be very helpful." She faltered slightly, "I have one other thing to ask you. Jill had the key to her condo in her suitcase, would it be too much of an imposition for you to check her condo for me? I really need to stay here for the next few days...."

She was close to tears again, and Moira quickly agreed. Joan stood up to fetch Ted's suitcase and Jill's key just as her husband came back into the room.

"We have an appointment with someone in the police department tomorrow morning. They want to bring the FBI in, they will be there too."

Joan left the room and quickly returned with the suitcase. She handed her Jill's apartment key, then unexpectedly put her arms around her and gave her a hug.

"Thank you for coming." She said.

Moira finished her drink quickly and said her goodbyes and they agreed to be in touch the next day after they had met with the authorities. Moira had brought an extra copy of the letter with her and now she handed it to them to give to the police. They thanked her again and Tom carried the suitcase out to her car. She backed out of the driveway and started the long trip back to Philadelphia, she was dead tired.

She drove back slowly. Traffic was still heavy and she kept to the inside lane – unusual for her, but tonight she did not feel that she was a hundred percent in control. Her thoughts wandered constantly, unfocused, and she felt nauseated. The meeting with Jill's parents had been harrowing and she had been deeply affected. She could not get them out of her head, Joan's panicked expression when she read the letter – the way they clung to each other, their palpable fear. In so many ways they reminded her of Jill – the same facial expressions and body language – how they moved…. It brought her own fears into sharp focus and she too was panicked for Jill's safety. Her disappearance was becoming very, very real and very frightening.

She was relieved when she finally reached her apartment building. She parked her car and took the elevator to her floor – not relaxing until she was inside her apartment with the door closed and locked behind her. She shed her business clothes and put on a robe. She had had nothing since breakfast apart from the vodka Tom had given her in Princeton. *Maybe eating something would help*…She scrambled a couple of eggs and sat down with the eggs and a glass of wine before she checked her messages……A lot of messages from people at work wanting to know how the meeting went with Jill's parents. *Jackals* she thought, and deleted them. Nothing from Jill. She remembered she had promised to call Dan, but couldn't face it tonight, she did not want to talk to anyone, she was going to bed, she'd call Dan tomorrow after she'd heard from Tom and Joan. They could talk about Ted's suitcase then too……

In New York it was gone seven o'clock by the time Dan left his office. It had taken him a while but he had finally located the corporate vice-president responsible for the division he headed, and as he had suspected he was out of the country – in China as it turned out. He sent him an email that Ted was dead, stating that the circumstances were unknown and that he would contact him again as soon as he knew more. He warned that the authorities might get involved as it had happened in England, but so far no one was aware what was going on. Just for the record he copied the Corporate Vice President for Human Resources. That done he took the elevator to the HR department, hoping that she was in her office and had time to talk. He was in luck – her door was open.

"Come in Dan, I was hoping you'd show up, I just read your email. What ever happened? Poor Ted, what a terrible shock, I'm so sorry, Dan, I know you and he were good friends."

"Thank you," he replied. "I'm still trying to process it; I wish I knew more."

He went on to tell her that he had only found out because Ted's friend had written a letter to a woman she worked with while she was still in England.

"And now," he added, "It appears that Ted's friend disappeared after she landed at JFK last Thursday night."

They talked for a while longer and she gave him the phone number of the next of kin Ted had designated. As Dan had thought, it was the uncle living in California. He promised to let her know as soon as he had more information and was getting up to leave when she spoke again.

"Interesting," she said scrolling down her computer screen, "He designated someone called Jill Davis as the beneficiary for the company life insurance plan. Do you know her? We should let her know too."

"Unfortunately she's the one who has disappeared." Dan said as he left.

He walked back to his office thinking about Ted. He could not believe that he was dead. The VP was correct, Ted is – *was* – he corrected himself – a good friend, remembering how concerned he had been for him when his marriage had broken up last year. At the time it had made him think that Ted had probably gone through something similar in his past… but he was very much his own person and very private, allowing only a few select people into his life. How the fuck had he got mixed up in this crazy thing? It was that off beat sense of humor of his…Jill shared a similar one, that's why answering that advertisement would have been a great joke to them. What the hell had happened? Two great people, they didn't deserve this…. *Please God let Jill show up!*

After he got back in his apartment he tried to call Ted's uncle in California, but got no answer. He left a brief message asking him to return his call then checked the time – he was supposed to be meeting friends but was in no mood to socialize with anyone and called to cancel. He wondered how the woman – *what was her name, Moira? –* was doing with her meeting with Jill's parents… He felt for her – that was a hard thing she had to do he thought, realizing it even more since trying to phone the uncle. *How do you tell someone that their nephew is dead? Christ!*

He had a restless evening, Moira had said she would call after she got back from Princeton, but it was getting very late and he realized it probably wasn't going to happen tonight.

He knew she must have had a difficult evening talking to Jill's parents, but still, she had said she would call, and it worried him – and irked him when he did not hear from her. It was new for him not to be in control, people came to him, it was rare that he had to reach out to them. If they said they would get back to him, they got back to him – and they got back when they said they would. He was used to being in charge. And he had hoped Moira would have some more information about Jill. He could not believe what was happening to his friends. He was very worried about Jill, and was still having a hard time wrestling with Ted's death. He decided he'd contact Moira tomorrow if he hadn't heard from her by the end of the day.

It was late and he turned in for the night.

TWELVE

Moira called Dan the next day around midday. She was sorry she hadn't called the night before, there hadn't been anything new to report and she had been exhausted when she got back from Princeton.

He was anxious to find out if there was any more news and told her there was no need to apologize, before quickly moving to ask about Jill's parents, were they all right, and was there anymore news?

"It was horrible." She said. "Their fear for Jill was palpable. As soon as he read the letter, Tom –her Father –went and called the police and they both were meeting with them, and the FBI, this morning. I just got off the phone with Tom – he called to let me know what happened."

She gave him a synopsis of his call. The police had put Jill's information into their data base and had already contacted the port authority who had confirmed that she had arrived on a flight from Heathrow on Thursday evening – and that the FBI were contacting the British authorities about both Ted's death and Jill's disappearance.

"By the way," she added, "We are probably going to be contacted by the guy from the FBI. His name is Mike Balmer."

"No news of Jill I suppose?" Dan asked.

"I'm afraid not – but there is one more thing. Ted's suitcase was delivered to them, I guess Jill had brought it back with her, and Joan – Jill's Mother – asked me if I could get it to you, apparently his notes from his business meetings in England are in it."

As an afterthought she added that probably the key to his apartment was in it too, if he wanted to take his things back to his apartment.

"Of course I'll take care of it," he said. Then added, "Jill's letter mentioned trying to find the list of phone numbers the guy from the ad had used. I'll look for that too while I'm there."

"Joan gave me Jill's key and asked me to check her condo." Moira told him. "I'm not looking forward to, but I promised I would."

They discussed how they could get Ted's suitcase to Dan and finally decided that Dan would catch a train to a station just outside Philadelphia, where Moira would meet him. He would re-arrange his schedule to be there the next day if Moira could make it.

"And if you would like some company, I'll come with you and we can check on Jill's apartment at the same time, then you can drop me back at the station." Dan suggested.

Moira was thankful for his offer, she had been dreading going by herself, and told him so.

Wednesday morning Moira drove to the station and pulled into one of the drop-off parking spaces in front of the platform just before the train was due.

It was a strange, awkward meeting. As she waited for the train it occurred to her that she had no idea what Dan looked like.

On the train the same thought had occurred to Dan. He reached for his phone and as the train pulled in he called her.

"How do I know you?"

"I'm standing by my car. I'm parked by the curb, just outside."

It was the typical small suburban train station, the morning commuter rush was over and only half a dozen people got off the train. She had no difficulty picking out which one was Dan – a tall man, late thirties to early forties with a shock of brown hair and an easy, confident walk. She waved and he came over to her.

"Moira?" He asked, shaking her hand. "Dan. Thanks for meeting me."

"Thank you for coming." She replied. "I am so sorry about Ted, I know he was your friend, and I'm so sorry I dropped it on you like that – I assumed you would have heard. I had no idea you didn't know ......"

He broke in. "There was no way you could have known. Let's just hope we find Jill soon."

He had changed the subject.

102

"Do you know Jill?" She asked.

"Yes, we used to go out to dinner with them quite a bit when they first got together."

"You're married?" More of a statement than a question from Moira…

"Not anymore." He replied wryly….

They drove in silence for fifteen minutes passing corporate buildings, shopping plazas, apartments, homes with well-groomed lawns, parks and numerous trees. *Typical suburban landscape Dan thought bitterly… Bad, bad Memories…*

"Here we are."

Moira turned into a pleasant condominium complex. Dan was surprised, for some reason he had pictured Jill living in a high rise apartment building. She saw his expression.

"She bought the townhouse last year, mainly because of the weekends with Ted I think. There are trails close by and they both like to run."

She pulled up in front of one of the townhouses. A thought that had been rumbling around in the back of her brain suddenly surfaced …. *Suppose we can't reach her because she's in there dead?....*

"Let's get this over with." She said. "I am really glad you're here, Dan, thank you for coming with me, I keep having a horrible thought that she may be in there, dead."

She got out the key to the front door and Dan took it from her.

"Let me go in first."

The apartment had the stuffy smell from being closed up for a week with the air conditioning off. She stayed by the door while Dan scanned the downstairs rooms then quickly went to the second floor and checked the bedrooms.

"She's not here." He said. "I'll wait for you in the kitchen."

Moira breathed out. *Thank God….*

She checked the apartment carefully. It was neat and tidy with abstract art and found trinkets scattered around. *Jill was organized and in a strange way – that's what allows her be a free spirit, Moira thought.* She went from room to room but found that Jill had left her apartment neat as a pin before she took off to join Ted in England. She returned to the kitchen area and Dan.

"Ready to go?" He pulled open the refrigerator door. "Need to do anything with this?"

She shook her head. "Let's go."

She locked the door and they got back in the car.

"Would you like to stop for coffee before I go back?" He asked.

She had seen him looking at his watch and shook her head.

"Not unless you do."

"I really should be getting back, there's a train at 1:15 – I can just about make it."

They reached the station with five minutes to spare. She popped the trunk and he lifted out Ted's suitcase.

"Let me know if you hear anything and I'll do the same."

He turned round and saw the strain in her face. He put the case down and put his arm around her shoulders.

"Are you going to be all right?"

The last thing she needed was sympathy – she moved back, away from any physical contact with him, but nodded and tried to give him a confident smile.

"Yes I think so, let's hope we get some good news soon."

The bell clanged announcing his train. He picked up Ted's case.

"Stay in touch." He said.

"You too." She replied.

He turned and strode across the platform to board the train.

She got back in her car to return to her office.

Both were glad to be alone, both of them needed space.

Moira had just settled back in her office when she got a call from Joan who was sobbing. Her heart sank, it had to be bad news…. Joan was barely coherent, but managed to pull herself together enough to tell her that the police had just contacted them to report that an unidentified woman's body had been found in Upper New York Bay several days earlier and that it could be Jill. Tom had gone into New York to meet with the Police.

"Oh, I'm so sorry, Joan. Would you like me to come there?"

"No, Moira, that's so kind of you but my sister and her husband will be here in a couple of hours – they are going to stay for a few days."

Moira was relieved, and she was glad that Joan would have the support of her sister. As an afterthought she added that she had given Ted's suitcase to Dan Murphy, and also that they had checked Jill's condo. She hung up the phone and leant back in her chair. She had a horrible feeling that Jill had been found. She thought about texting Dan, but couldn't get herself to do it. *Wait until you hear for sure* she told herself. The phone call from Joan had thrown her. It had brought her fears for Jill into sharp reality … *There's no way I can do any work …. I have to get out of here…* She was close to panic. Down the elevator – *forget the stairs* she didn't want to meet anyone. Out through the lobby – a hike across several parking areas and she was at her car. She got in and started driving. She had no idea where she was going, she just wanted to keep moving. *Let the car pick the route….* She drove through the green lights, turned right if the light was red, turned left if there was a green arrow and changed lanes to avoid lines of traffic …. *Anything to avoid stopping, must keep moving. …..*

When things started to register again, she found she was doing eighty miles an hour on a wide open highway on her way to Atlantic City. She hated Atlantic City so as soon she could she turned onto the Garden State Parkway and headed south along the Jersey Shore. Thirty miles on she saw the exit for Stone Harbor and on an impulse took it. She remembered Jill telling her how she and her parents spent two weeks in Stone Harbor every summer when she was growing up. She headed for the beach, paid the day fee and went down close to the water. It was a beautiful day, school was out but it was the middle of the week and the beach was not crowded. She walked for a while, then headed into the edge of the sand dunes and sat down on the warm sand facing the ocean. She needed to sort out her thoughts. But she could not stop seeing Jill as a child playing on the beach – happy – paddling in the water – picking up shells. She started to cry, the tears came, unwelcome, unstoppable and she covered her eyes with her hands and sobbed. *God! Poor Jill…* Moira was scared for her. *Who had grabbed her?… Why? … What the hell was going on? … Who were these people?…. Please God let them be caught! …. Please God let someone find out what is going on ……*

105

Her thoughts turned to Tom and Joan, what must they be going through? Jill was their only child. It made here think about her own parents, *if anything ever happened to Alistair or me it would destroy them.* Her parents had been in her thoughts a lot since her visit to Princeton.

She stayed on the beach until most of the day trippers had left for home, then got back in her car and headed back to Philadelphia and reached her apartment just as the light started to fade…

It was well after nine o'clock when her cell phone rang and she recognized the Princeton number. She answered, and heard an unfamiliar male voice on the other end. He identified himself as Tom's brother-in-law. He was calling for Tom and Joan because they had received very bad news. It was Jill's body in the morgue, Tom had identified her. He added that there was even more stress because the authorities were insisting on an autopsy and inquest before they would release her body.

"Tom wanted me to let you know that Jill has been found, and also to warn you that as the recipient of Jill's letter, you would be one of the people called to testify at the inquest, you will get the official notice once it has been scheduled."

She thanked him and asked him to give Joan and Tom her sympathy and her love, and managed to end the call still in control of her emotions. *What to do now? What was going on?* This sort of thing happened to other people, not anyone in her circle, not to Jill. She did not want to think about the hell she must have gone through… But Moira was glad there was going to be an inquest. Maybe now they would actually believe what Jill and Ted had being trying to tell everyone.....

Jill was dead. Until that last call she had clung to the desperate hope that she was still alive. She got up from the sofa, poured herself a scotch then sat down again, put her drink on the coffee table, and called her parents. She knew she would feel better after she had talked to them, she always did. Growing up she and her brother Alistair had often champed at the bit at their parents' careful approach to Life. "Too Scottish!" They fumed, but long term their method of child raising had served them both well. Their parents had emigrated from Scotland after the end of the Second World War. Newlyweds, they wanted to start their married life in a young country with the promise of greater opportunities. Like many others at that time, they had fled the hardships and grey misery of Britain in the late 1940's and settled in Ontario, in the town of Hamilton. There they had found a young community of like souls from all parts of war torn Europe fleeing the aftermath of the war that had ravaged their countries. They would joke that it was hard to find any true Canadians, everyone was a transplant. Years later Moira figured out that they were the fabric that had built modern day Canada – by that time though, she was firmly ensconced in the States, only going back to Canada for the holidays after attending college in Ann Arbor.

That night, talking to her parents she urgently felt the need to return to the security of her childhood in Canada. So now she told them everything that was going on, how Jill was dead, and Jill's friend Ted was dead, and about Jill's letter, and that there was going to be an inquest and that she was going to have to be a witness, how everything was totally unreal, and very upsetting... And that she missed them and wished she was there so they could talk. Her reaction surprised her – and her parents. It was unlike her to back away from anything. As she knew they would, they told her to stick it out, that she could handle it and that it was the least she could do for her friend Jill. She needed to stay until everything was resolved. After it was over they hoped she could get away for at least a weekend to visit them and relax.

"And of course, we'll be seeing you at Christmas, eh?" Her Mother added.

Moira promised to call again very soon.

She felt a bit calmer. She sat back on the sofa...*What next?* Then she remembered ... *Damn, I have to let Dan know!*

She didn't want to have to talk, to him or anyone else any more that night, so sent him a text, *Jill's body found in NY Bay. There's going to be an inquest.*

Five minutes later her phone rang. It was Dan, wanting to find out more. "Not much more I can tell you." She said, and gave him the sparse details she knew.

"That's a real bummer," he said sadly. "I was so hoping she would be found alive."

She suddenly remembered he was suffering the loss of not one, but two friends and in his own way was suffering as much as she was......

"Listen." He said. "One more thing. My VP wants me to join him in China to wrap up the details of his meetings... normally Ted would have gone so now I have to fill in ...."

"I'll send you a text if I hear anything." She broke in.

"Thank you for that... I'm afraid I won't have time to take Ted's suitcase to his apartment until I get back, I hope that's O.K? ..."

He voiced a new concern. "But now Jill's been found dead, maybe we should let the FBI know about the case. I figured the British authorities went through it after Ted died, but Jill's death changes things. I'll leave it in my office if anyone needs it."

She told him she would take care of it, and wished him a safe trip.

"I'll probably be back in about ten days." He said. "We'll talk when I get back."

They ended their call.

He went to pack for his trip, she to finish her scotch.

THIRTEEN

Thursday she was up early ready to face the day. *If Dan can focus enough to go to China, I can certainly focus on what I have to do today.* She reached the office and as usual went to the security desk to check in.

"Hey Moira!" One of the security staff called out. "You forgot to turn in your badge last night."

She fished it out of her bag and hung it around her neck.

"Sorry." She said.

"Please don't forget again." He said and signed her in. "Someone was asking for you earlier, but he didn't want me to call your department – he said he would wait."

She looked around at the people in the reception area and asked, "Which one is him? What is his name? What does he look like?"

"He didn't want to give his name or company so I asked him to leave. He was medium height, probably late forties, dark hair, business suit – usual visitor type." He replied.

He pressed the button allowing her through to the atrium and for once Moira was glad the Company had installed aggressive security. Maybe it was the guy from the FBI she thought – she hoped she was right.

Up in her office she put the finishing touches to the presentation she was making the following day in Washington. Originally she had scheduled the presentation for a Friday so she could meet her friends who lived in Georgetown and then spend the weekend with them on the Delaware Coast. It all seemed so insignificant now…… She met with the members of her team for a final run through and apologized for not being available the day before. She offered no explanation, and nobody asked for one... they were handling her with kid gloves. Everyone seemed to know about Jill. She buried herself in her work and found it a relief to be able to concentrate on something concrete.

Near the end of the day her phone rang and the man on the other end of the line identified himself as Michael Balmer from the FBI. She was about to ask him if he had visited her office that morning when caution overcame her and she made an excuse that someone was in her office, asked for his number, and said she would get back in ten minutes. She googled the number recorded on her phone against the information that Tom had given her before calling him back.

"Sorry about that." She said. "Tom Davis told me you would be contacting me."

He got right down to the reason he was calling. They needed to get together. What was the best time for her to meet him tomorrow? Looking at the presentation still incomplete on her desk she told him that tomorrow she had to be in Washington for work.

"That's better for me," he replied. "That's where my office is. What time will your meetings be over?"

They agreed to meet at 4:00 pm and he gave her directions to his office. She was in for a long day, but she was happy that at last someone was investigating Jill's story, and was eager to meet with him. She had forgotten to tell him about the man who had showed up at her office who wouldn't give his name. *It was probably nothing...* but she must remember to do that tomorrow....

In Washington the next day the presentation to the pharmaceutical company went well. Supposedly she was the team leader, but today her team carried her, and she was very grateful. Her thoughts were racing ahead, anticipating her meeting with the FBI. Their meetings wrapped up by the middle of the afternoon which gave her ample time to drive to Georgetown and leave her car near her friends' apartment.

From Georgetown she took a cab to the FBI building on Pennsylvania Avenue. Michael Balmer *("Call me Mike" he had said on the phone)* had told her which entrance to use and that he would meet her in the lobby.

She arrived in plenty of time and checked in with the reception desk, letting them know she was meeting with Michael Balmer at four, then found a chair and sat down to wait.

It wasn't long before a man came out of the elevator and the woman at the desk pointed him in her direction. She stood up as he crossed the lobby towards her. He was not like she had imagined. A real pyknic type she thought, maybe a couple of inches taller than her, but probably not six foot, a thick physique tending towards chubby, short thick neck below a lively face, curly dark hair and intense eyes. Very charming and very Irish she thought …. probably a lot of fun but unreliable outside of work.

"Moira?" He grinned and held out his hand. "Mike. Come on there's a conference room near here, we can talk there."

She followed him down a corridor until he opened one of the doors and ushered her into a room dominated by a large conference table. They sat down in adjoining chairs at one end.

"Room to spread out." He joked to put her at ease. "OK, I have a copy of the letter Jill Davis sent you and would like to go through it with you."

For the next half hour he questioned her about the letter, what she knew about Jill, and what she knew about Ted – and also what she knew about Dan Murphy. She told him about her friendship with Jill, that she had met her at work and that they had shared similar interests but added that she had only met Ted once, and knew very little about him.

"Jill and Ted were very private people and Jill was not the type to talk about their relationship. She had been excited about going to join him in England. That's all I know."

She paused, "And about Dan Murphy – I believe he was Ted's boss, but after I met him I realized that he and Ted and Jill were also friends. I contacted his office last Monday when we were trying to find Jill. I had remembered his name from the evening when Jill and Ted and I went out for drinks, but had never met him or talked to him before then. And I met him for the first time two days ago when he picked up Ted's suitcase from me. Jill's mother had asked me to get it to Dan because the papers from Ted's business trip were in it, and at the time it seemed like the best thing to do. And Dan said he could get it back to Ted's apartment. That was when we were still hoping Jill would be found, before we knew she was dead. In retrospect we should have thought to give the case to you. I'm sorry about that."

"Do you know where Dan is?" Mike asked. "I haven't been able to reach him."

"He's in China on a business trip. He should be back in about ten days."

"Do you know where Ted's suitcase is?"

Dan told me that he hadn't had time to take it to Ted's apartment yet, he said he was going to leave it in his office."

Mike was wrapping up the meeting, "You've given me a lot to follow up on." He said. "Anything else you can tell me?"

She suddenly remembered to tell him about the man who had come to her work.

"Yes." She said. "Yesterday a man showed up at my company and asked to speak to me. He wouldn't give his name or his company so Security asked him to leave."

Mike looked serious. She gave him the vague description she had been given and the name of the security guard who talked to him.

"I'll check it out." He said.

He escorted her back to the lobby making small talk about the coming weekend as they walked. At the entrance, he turned towards her

"I'll be back in touch." He said.

They shook hands and Moira left.

She headed back to Georgetown to meet her friends and gave them a brief rundown about what was going on before trying to push it all to the back of her mind. She wanted to forget about everything – about Jill and Ted being dead, and about the man who had showed up at her office – and hoped that for a little while the weekend at the Delaware Shore would help her do just that. Her friends belonged to a group of thirty-somethings who had leased a large Victorian House close to the beach for the summer, and this was their turn to invite their friends to the shore. Moira had been there before and was used to the amorphous group of people who would come and go throughout the weekend. Lots of people and partying was the usual outcome, but occasionally there would be the chance to have a decent conversation or meet someone new. It was a welcome relief to get away from the current turmoil.

Saturday was a beautiful day and everyone spent a lazy time on the beach before picking up pizzas and heading back to the house, and it wasn't long before people started arriving bearing beer or wine for the evening's festivities. Most knew each other, many of them part of similar summer rentals, and they would get together most weekends. The party was in full swing when two more party-goers appeared at the door.

"Hey, is there a Moira Gregory here?" One called out.

She raised her arm and waved.

"There's a guy out there asking for you." He said.

"What does he look like?" She asked, suddenly remembering the man who had showed up at her company.

"Too old for you, my darling, close to fifty." He joked. "I asked him for his name and he left. I guess I scared him off…"

Her stomach lurched and all her fears roared to the surface again. What should she do now? *Was she being targeted by the same people who had killed Jill and Ted? … Was she a threat? … Why? What did they think she knew?* All she wanted to do was find out why her friends were dead. She had to call Mike… She found an empty room upstairs, and let the phone ring for a long time. No answer. – And no voicemail either. She tried texting him but he did not get back.

She felt very alone – and abandoned. Mike had told her to contact him if the man showed up again and had made her believe that he would be there if she needed him. It made her re-think her confidence in him…. *Was he reliable? … Had he just been pacifying her……After all she'd only met him once….* It made her question her own judgement and it undermined her confidence.

Out of the window she could see the beach in the distance, only one lonely figure wandered along the shore – normally she would have found some friends to go for a swim, but not tonight, she was too afraid. She pulled herself together and went downstairs back to the party.

It had to have been a good hour later when the same guest – who hadn't made it much beyond the door except to replenish his drink – called out again. "Hey Moira, you're popular tonight, John's here asking for you."

She looked around and saw Mike Balmer, now in beach clothes with a 'Hail fellow well met' swagger. She felt a wave of relief.

"Moira me darling." He said as he came across the room towards her "Alistair said he wouldn't forgive me if I didn't look you up while I'm here."

He threw his arms around her and gave her an enthusiastic hug, then whispered in her ear, "My name's John Flaherty, play along."

She leant back so she could look into his face.

"What a surprise, John!" She gave him a genuine grin. "It's so good to see you, and how is my dear brother?"

"Let me get a drink, then I'll catch you up."

He grabbed her hand, and steered her to a quiet corner, snatching up a beer as he passed a table. They sat close together like long lost family friends and he asked her if she thought the man who had tried to crash the party was the same one who had shown up at her workplace. She didn't know for sure but the description was the same. He told her not to worry, his colleague was keeping an eye on him. She could feel herself relax.

"How did you know where I was?" She asked.

"There's no small talk in my business, do you remember us talking about our weekend plans? More than enough information for me to figure out where you would be – I was concerned about the man who showed up at your work – and also I figured he just might be the lead I needed – Oh, and I did see your text just now... Now," he said, "I'm off to meet the revelers." Then as an afterthought, "Just remember I'm an old family friend."

She watched him go back into the party flirting outrageously with all of the women, talking with a thick Irish brogue. *Damn he's good he's really enjoying this* she thought watching him work the room.

A woman came up to her. "Why did you let that one get away?"

"Too many family ties." She answered and moved to another group.

The party was starting to wind down when Mike/a.k.a John sauntered across the room to Moira.

"Listen Moira, I'm going to stay here tonight." The brogue had disappeared and he was suddenly serious.

"Is the man still around? I thought you said you had it under control, what's happened?" She was visibly upset.

"This guy has tried to get to you twice, we can't arrest him because we have nothing on him yet, we're building a case, but right now we can only watch him. And he's not working alone... Anyway, I'm staying here tonight, I can sleep anywhere."

The last guests finally left and Mike settled himself on the sofa.

"See you in the morning, girls." He said, and purposefully closed his eyes.

It was light when Moira woke up, but very early and everyone was still asleep. She crept downstairs so as not to wake them. Mike was not on the sofa, it upset her that he had gone, but hoped it meant her stalker had left the area. She tried to put all thoughts of stalkers out of her head.... The house had that after party smell of stale pizza and liquor – it did not sit well .... She started some coffee and then went around the room gathering up the paper plates and empty bottles until the coffee was ready. She poured herself a cup and was about to take it out on the porch when she realized Mike was sitting in one of the wicker chairs talking on his phone. She poured a second cup and pushed open the screen door to the porch. He finished his call when he saw her coming and she handed him one of the coffees.

"It's black, do you take anything in it?"

"It's fine just like it is." He replied.

She sat down in an adjoining chair, waking up slowly. She never wanted to talk in the mornings and today was no exception, particularly after the party the night before. She sat watching the sun breaking through the mist, drinking her coffee. *It was obscene to think about the horrible things that were going on when it promised to be such a beautiful day.* Mike's voice broke into her thoughts telling her that he was about to be picked up by a colleague, but that she would be seeing him again soon. She opened her mouth to speak just as his ride pulled up. He got up from his chair, and gave her a friendly kiss.

"Thanks for the coffee, I'll see you soon."

Then he ran down the steps into the waiting car.

FOURTEEN

Moira had a hard time settling back into work on Monday. She had hoped that her weekend on the shore would help her forget for a little while all the tragic events that had taken place recently – and it had been working until that man showed up again. She wished Dan was around, he knew the history, and Ted and Jill were his friends too. Thank God that Mike – *or should she think of him as John?* –had showed up. Her friends had teased her mercilessly but she had kept his cover intact, insisting that he was just her brother's friend…. She wondered how Dan was doing in China and thought she really should email him – but what was there to say?

By mid-week Moira felt things were almost normal and she was finally getting back into the work routine. But then a couple of incidents brought everything back to the new reality. On Wednesday morning as she walked across the lobby to check in, a man's voice from behind whispered in her ear.
"Did you have a good time at the shore? I hope you get a chance to go down again before the summer ends. Nice to see you again."
She turned, and saw the back of a man walking towards the revolving door. She ran to the Security desk.
"Go after that man! Quickly!"

They moved fast, but by the time they reached the entrance there was no sign of him. They ran on out into the grounds. Harry, the head of security, came back to her.

"They probably won't catch him, there was a car just leaving the visitors parking and he probably had someone waiting to pick him up."

She had to reach Mike. Once in her office she texted him letting him know the man had shown up at her work again.

The second thing happened the same morning. Her phone rang. It was the New York coroner's office requesting her presence at Jill's inquest. It would be held in approximately ten days; this was advance notice to inform her she must make herself available to give testimony. She would be getting detailed information in the mail with the date, time and location.

Mike returned her text a little later. *"Meeting Harry from Security at 12. Lunch after?"*

They agreed to meet in the cafeteria after his meeting.

He got there before her and found a seat where he could watch the stairs, and as usual spent the wait answering texts and emails. He was never idle. He looked up and saw her coming, winding her way down the spiral stairs from the fourth floor. *Those stairs would keep you in shape all by themselves* he thought as he watched her coming down. Automatically he noted her appearance. She was attractive, early thirties, trim body, around 5.8" or 5.9" he thought. Very Scottish face, thin nose in a thin face and that unruly flaming ginger hair! He had warmed to her from their first meeting and liked the way she handled herself. He knew she was under a lot of stress, he could see it in her walk....

They greeted each other formally – this was work for both of them. Then he grinned.

"How are you holding up, Moira Gregory?" He asked.

"A little un-nerved, thank you Mr.... What should I call you today?" She queried.

"Mike." He said seriously. "So that bastard showed up again, eh? Harry and I had a good meeting, let's get our food and sit down then we can talk."

Once at a table she opened the conversation again.

"Your meeting with Harry?"

"Very helpful." He answered. "For what it's worth, I think they're just trying to intimidate you, they've had plenty of opportunity to do you harm before now."

"Thanks a lot!" She said sarcastically, "Well they're certainly succeeding, whatever they have in mind."

He hoped his assessment was correct but he did not want to alarm her any more than was necessary. He would make it a priority to get the men stalking her into custody as quickly as possible and made a mental note… *stay close enough to protect her.*

Moira had many questions. She wanted to know why they were stalking her, how many people were in the organization, and what was their aim, and why were Ted and Jill killed? How was the investigation going? Mike answered her questions vaguely, giving her no details but told her they were making progress. He kept to himself his frustrations … *It was still early …connections would be coming faster soon…. they always gathered speed once the basic structure was solid…. The handful of members they had identified so far appeared to have no commonality – no common focus, no common history.* Out-loud he added that he wished Dan was in town so they could get together, and he wanted to get hold of Ted's case, it might hold more information from Ted, but for this stage of the investigation things were going well.

He changed the subject.

"I enjoyed your party last Saturday."

She grinned. "That was obvious!" She said, "You really know how to work a room."

"Ah! I love my work." He replied.

"You really do, don't you? Love your work I mean."

"I really do." He replied, suddenly serious. "It's all consuming, always different, I love it, it's my very demanding mistress – and I'm totally hooked."

They had almost finished lunch and Moira had been thinking. She was feeling guilty about the suitcase. it had made sense to her when Joan had asked her to take the case with Ted's business papers from his UK trip back to his boss – and friend – Dan, because at the time everyone was still hopeful that Jill would show up. It was only after they knew she was dead that it had occurred to her and Dan that the FBI would want to get hold of it... And then of course, Dan had had to leave for China unexpectedly....

"About the case." She said. Did you call Dan's office? He said he'd leave it there."

"I did, but it wasn't there."

Damn! Ma*ybe he'd taken it to Ted's apartment after all.* She wracked her brains to think of something more she could do.

"Would it help if you could get into Ted's apartment before Dan gets back? I mean, without having to break the door down or anything? Maybe Jill had a spare key at her place, they always spent the weekend either at her place or his and I still have Jill's key, I'll go over there after work and look for one."

"Could you go now?" Mike asked, "I'll come with you."

She looked at the time. "If we do it fast. It's not far."

She drove, she knew the way and it was quicker. On the way over she told him about the call from New York that morning requesting her at the inquest.

"Will you be giving evidence too?" She asked him.

"No, I won't even be there." He replied. "The police and the FBI like to keep their investigations separate, and right now I'd like to keep it that way. Too many opportunities for leaks.... And please don't say anything about me or the FBI – or anything about the man who keeps showing up – that's not relevant to them reaching a decision about why your friend died – however frustrated you might be at their conclusions."

She asked what he meant and he replied that the police would have a very different focus on the evidence.

"All they are looking at is the reason Jill's body was found in New York Bay." He said. Then added, "And be prepared, you may not agree with their conclusions."

She promised to keep him and the FBI out of the answers she gave – although she was not sure she agreed with his philosophy....

It was obvious that no one had been in the apartment since she and Dan were there. Jill's parents had not been over and now Moira regretted not cleaning out the refrigerator the first time as Dan had suggested. But then she still was clinging to the hope that Jill was alive and didn't want to jinx it by throwing out the food....

"God, I'd better clean out the refrigerator, I can't let Joan face that when she comes here. Hey Mike, I know you're an expert searcher, can you start to look for the key?"

She needn't have bothered to ask, Mike was already opening drawers and rifling through papers on Jill's desk. She left him to his search.

She found a trash bag and started tossing rotting vegetables, molding cheese and half used bottles of sauces into it. Then she checked the freezer and emptied out the ice cubes but decided to leave everything else as it was. It did not take long – Jill had expected to be away for the week and the refrigerator was almost empty. She closed the doors and looked around for Mike. He had almost completed a systematic search of the whole apartment and came back into the kitchen empty-handed. Suddenly his face lit up. She was still standing by the refrigerator and he came towards her – then leant in and reached behind her left ear triumphantly grabbing a key ring from a magnetic hook attached to the side of the refrigerator.

"Bingo!" He said. "I missed this before because the refrigerator door was open. Let's see what we have here."

There were four keys on the ring – one was obviously a mailbox key. They checked the other three. One opened the front door, but the other two remained a mystery. Mike removed them from the ring and handed Moira the ring with the mailbox and front door key. He pocketed the other two.

"I'm going to keep these for now, I'm hoping we get lucky and one of them is to Ted's apartment, I'll make sure I get them back to you so you can get them to Jill's parents."

He looked around the apartment again then picked up the trash bag. "Come on, let's get back." He said. "We'll check her mailbox on the way out."

They locked up and put the trash out at the curb then looked for Jill's mailbox and found it close by in the cul-de-sac with the rest of the boxes for the section. Mike sorted the mail as they drove back and found that Jill had sent herself a copy of the letter she had sent to

Moira. It had an additional note scrawled across the top. Mike read it to Moira as she drove.

"I think my car is bugged ... I'm leaving here. No GPS and I'll go the back way over the moors. I hope I'm just being paranoid..."

"Poor Jill." Moira said very quietly.

"Amen." Mike replied.

He sighed. "Damn I wish I could talk to Dan and find Ted's case."

Moira felt the need to say something encouraging.

"Let's hope one of the keys gets you into his apartment, maybe you'll find something there."

They lapsed into silence.

FIFTEEN

In China, Dan was not enjoying his unscheduled trip. It appeared that all of his Chinese counterparts knew and liked Ted and were very upset at his demise and Dan spent a lot of his time accepting their sympathy and fielding their questions. The work was difficult too. Ted had been a genius at the final fine tuning of contracts with all the attention to minute details it required. It was not Dan's forte and was an added burden to all the emotions he was currently feeling. Apart from daily emails from his division, he heard from no one. He felt isolated and far from where he wanted to be. And abandoned, no contact or information from anyone – he had thought that at least Moira would have been in touch... Finally, after a week with no news he sent her a message *"Any news? What's going on?"*

His message showed up on Moira's phone late Wednesday evening. She remembered that China was eleven hours ahead of the east coast and for Dan it was already halfway through Thursday. She emailed him that there were no answers yet – that the inquest was in about eight days and she had to give testimony. She was being stalked but hopefully Mike the FBI guy had it under control, and that Mike wanted to talk with him as soon as he was back in New York. And where was Ted's case?

Dan replied immediately *Thanks for getting back, I feel totally out of touch and unfortunately the end is not in sight yet. Everybody was used to working with Ted and his name and past work is referred to constantly. I'm finding it hard going. My Ex has Ted's case. She was to pick up some items I had left for her at the office and for some*

unfathomable reason the receptionist gave her the case as well... I don't like the sound of you being stalked, please stay safe. Is this Mike- guy any good?
Wish I was there to give you support.
Best, Dan.
From Moira: *Is there any way I can retrieve the case from your Ex? What's her address? Sorry your trip is so difficult – it can't be easy having them bringing up Ted so much.*
Hang in there. Moira
It was very late and Moira went to bed.

She found an email from Dan with the Ex's address on Thursday morning when she woke up. She forwarded it to Mike. An hour later she got an automated response from his email. *Out of the country. Will contact you when I return.*
Damn! She thought - what should I do now?... Why does he always have to be unavailable when I really need to talk to him? She realized that she was beginning to think of him as her safety blanket and did not like the sensation, but it didn't stop her wondering where he had gone and how soon he would get back.

Mike was striding along the edge of a cliff on the North Devon coast in a driving rain leaning into a gale force wind which was almost blowing him off his feet.
"I thought this was supposed to be summer," he muttered."
His companion laughed. "This was your idea – you have to see everything for yourself is what you said."
"I didn't order this weather though." Mike said through gritted teeth...
He was walking with his English counterpart – a hulking man from the area, who was used to the wild coastal storms and who was getting a great deal of satisfaction from Mike's discomfort.
They walked in silence to the end of the Coastal Path and then turned down the small dangerous trail leading to the very end of the land. In good weather it was treacherous, but today it was downright foolhardy to attempt it. They took their time and climbed down the path cut into the side of the cliff with extreme care. In places the trail had broken

away completely and Mike looked down at the roaring waves lashing the rocks far below. *Christ this was stupid he thought, I need to buy Jim a drink when we get back...* They finally reached the flat grassy area at the edge of the cliff. Only the angry grey Atlantic Ocean before them with gigantic waves crashing onto the rocks far below throwing flecks of foam way up in the air. The noise was deafening. Mike found the driving rain and the wind and the deafening roar of the waves exhilarating. He loved storms. He was awed by the power of Nature.

Jim came up close to him and yelled into his ear trying to make himself heard above the wind and waves. "Don't go too close to the edge, it's very unstable!"

This time Mike heeded the warning. OK he'd seen for himself where Ted had gone over the cliff and in good weather it probably wasn't an accident. The edge of the cliff where it had happened was not undermined he could see it was solid, and flat....

"Come on, let's get back!" He yelled above the noise, "I need a drink – I'm buying."

"The least you can do!" His companion yelled back.

Jim knew exactly which pub Mike would select and sure enough forty minutes later they were five miles back along the coast in the warmth of the old pub near the church. They went up to the bar.

"It's bloody cold, I need some scotch, what are you having?" Mike asked Jim.

Jim ordered the same and noticed that Mike had suddenly developed a distinct Irish accent....

"Two doubles." Mike ordered from the woman behind the bar, then engaged her in conversation.

"Me friend was here a couple of months ago and he told me to be sure to give his regards to the guy behind the bar, when will he be here?"

The woman drew into herself and became serious.

"Some bastard ran him off the road." She answered. "He's still in the hospital."

Mike made himself a mental note *get the report, go to the hospital.*

"Oh God, I'm sorry." He said. "Please wish him well for me."

They took their drinks to a small table close to the fire – they were both soaking wet and glad of the heat. They talked quietly together and set their schedules for the next day. Mike planned to visit the hotel on the cliffs where Ted and Jill had stayed and then visit the hospital. He needed Jim to find out who he should talk to about the military base on the Burrows and how to get access there and then run down the police reports about the bartender's accident.

Back in the States Moira was focusing on what she could do to move the investigation along. She was still feeling bad that she had not realized the importance of the suitcase earlier. It was only after they'd had lunch in the cafeteria that it had sunk in just how much Mike wanted to get hold of it. Finally she had sensed his urgency – she felt dumb not to have seen it before. She had tried to make amends. She had found out where the case was and had passed the information on to Mike – only to find he was out of the country... *For God know how long. ... What should she do now? ... How could she speed things along?...*
By early afternoon she had decided, and made her plans. It was already Thursday so she picked up the phone and called Dan's Ex. The call was a little frosty, but the Ex agreed to let Moira pick up Ted's case. She learnt that the Ex's name was Holly, and they agreed on a mutual time. That coming Saturday at 2.00 p.m.
Then she texted Mike her plan....

In the pub Mike's phone vibrated and he dug it out of his pocket. It was a text from Moira. *Going to pick up T's case on Saturday.*
He exploded. "Shit!" And answered her text: *Don't be bloody stupid! Wait!*
Moira got Mike's text but ignored it. She was furious.
"Problem?" Jim asked.
"This crazy woman who worked with Jill is going to pick up the missing suitcase on Saturday. Doesn't she realize it's dangerous?"
"Maybe she doesn't." Jim offered casually.
Mike looked at him, calming down.
"You're probably right – but she won't change her mind. She knows they're following her but she'll just stick out her chin and toss her ginger hair and go anyway. She's that type."

He sent Moira another text. *Please wait, it could be dangerous. Do not go. Back next week.*

How patronizing! She thought…. He doesn't think I'm capable of doing anything. I'm going… But this time she answered his text. *Don't worry I'll be careful.*

Mike had summed up her response correctly. For once he wished he had been wrong. He had a short fuse when anything interfered with his plan of action – and Moira's actions not only disrupted his plans, but also gave him the added worry of keeping her safe – even though she had put herself in danger. *Willfully,* to his mind. He had begun to realize that he could not control her actions – especially from the other side of the Atlantic. A nagging thought kept on returning that he might have underestimated the danger to her. It worried him. He was angry on both accounts.

"I have to make some calls…" He said.

SIXTEEN

On Saturday Moira set off early to make sure she got to Holly's address on time. She had the distinct feeling that if she was ten minutes late Holly would have purposely gone out... She got onto I- 95 and was soon in New Jersey.

Was she being paranoid or had there been a black jeep following her ever since she left her apartment? She cursed Mike for putting a bug in her ear – *Did he think there was danger around every corner* – she decided to ignore it. Near Bridgewater she turned onto I-287. She could have gone her old familiar way using the state roads, but she wanted to make sure she wasn't held up by traffic, and besides, she wanted to see if that annoying black jeep followed.... It did. All the way up 287 she kept glancing back, watching the jeep in her rear view mirror, but when she followed her GPS instructions to turn off at exit 37 and the jeep followed – and it followed her when she turned left at the fork in the road – she got nervous. She was in a community about five miles away from her destination, on a wide suburban road, on one side, small houses, trees and the township's offices. On the other, a recreation complex with ball parks and tennis courts and next to them – *thank God* – a police station! She turned into the carpark. The black jeep followed....

She didn't know whether to stay in her car and lay on the horn, or get out and run like hell into the building. She was opening her car door when her phone rang. She answered it and a male voice told her to look out of her window. She looked up and saw a young man with long blond hair in the black jeep which was parked two spaces away. He had rolled down his window and was pointing to the FBI badge he was holding up. "Can I come over? You can stay in your car and keep the engine running if you like."

She closed the car door without getting out and locked it, then cracked the window. He sauntered over, a tall lanky kid in cut-off jeans and a tee. She figured he was twenty-five years old, tops.

"Mike told me to keep an eye on you," he said.

"What proof do you have? You look very young to be FBI."

"Yeah, I just finished my training," he said with a grin. "I can show you Mike's text if you like?"

He scrolled through his phone until he found what he wanted and handed her his phone.

"Excuse what he says about you, he was upset."

Moira rolled the window all the way down and read the text. *"That stupid woman is picking up T's case on Sat. Don't let her the fuck out of your sight. Keep her safe."*

"I don't think he meant for you to sit on my bumper," she said sarcastically. "I saw you almost as soon as I drove out of my garage."

"I'd rather make you angry than make Mike angry." He answered grinning. "I'll get better."

She looked at the time and started up her car.

"I'd better get going. Are you going to follow me again? How will you know when I start back?"

He looked sheepish.

"Actually there's a tracking device on your car." He said. "Sorry."

Holly lived in the next town over. Well known for its great schools and great community it was home to many of the executives employed by the corporations scattered around northern New Jersey– and it was a haven for commuters, New York City was under an hour away via New Jersey transit. She visualized Dan all dressed up for work catching the train every morning and evening. *Ugh, she thought, I bet he hated it!*

Her GPS guided her through the center of the town and finally directed her to turn left into a large townhouse complex. The buildings were grouped around a small lake with a fountain in the middle. A circular road enclosed the whole community and located at the back, the usual amenities; the club house adjoining the swimming pool, tennis courts and a dog park. Holly's townhouse faced the lake. Moira rang the bell and heard footsteps coming to door. It opened and a slim blond woman stood in the doorway.

"Right on time." She said with ice in her voice. "You must be Dan's new squeeze. I'll get the case."

"Excuse me!" Moira interrupted. "You have the wrong idea. I've only met Dan once, to give him Ted's case, I'm sorry you thought that."

Holly bent slightly, "I'm sorry." She said. "Come in."

She led Moira into a pleasant living room. Two over-stuffed pale yellow loveseats faced each other across a long, low coffee table, white carpet on the floor. Out of the picture window, the lake shimmered. *Very House and Garden Moira thought.*

Holly offered Moira some tea.

"Can you tell me what's going on?" She asked.

It turned out Holly had known nothing until the receptionist at Dan's office had handed her Ted's suitcase.

Moira filled her in with all she knew, and that the police and the FBI were trying to get answers about why Ted and Jill had died.

Holly was very upset.

"I can't believe it! Dan and I would go out with them quite a lot when they first got together. They were a lovely couple and we were so happy for them." She paused, "Then of course, Dan and I broke up..." She finished bitterly.

Moira kept quiet, she did not want to hear any more. She saw that Holly was totally bound up in her own raw misery....

She left with the case safely in the trunk of her car and headed for the entrance to I-287 South. She was glad to be on the road heading back home. She glanced in her rear view mirror and grinned as the black jeep came down the ramp onto the highway several cars behind her. There was not much traffic on the road and she would make good time.

She had travelled about fifteen miles when she looked back and saw a red pick-up truck coming up fast behind her in the middle lane. She moved to the inside lane to let it pass – and realized it didn't mean to

129

pass but was about to follow her into the same lane. It was then that she saw the black jeep suddenly accelerate, flying up the inside lane until he was right behind her, close to her bumper leaving no space for the red pickup to get between them... But now the jeep was in the middle and she watched in the rearview mirror with mounting horror as the red pickup truck turned its wheels more and more into the jeep. She could see that her young FBI friend was talking, and hoped he was calling for backup. It was obvious the red pickup was determined to push the jeep off the road. Moira was scared, she called 911 and gave their location and yelled for them to hurry. If it went on much longer she knew the pickup would succeed – and probably clip her and send her spinning into the oncoming traffic as well. They were travelling at high speed but there was no way they could outrun the pickup which continued to turn into the jeep. Somehow the jeep managed to stay on the road, the young FBI agent was driving masterfully.

Finally the truck dropped away... then came roaring back turning its wheels sharply into the side of the jeep and like a bull dozer kept pushing until the jeep turned over and over down the embankment, but the truck could not straighten out in time and followed the jeep, bouncing down the steep incline finally crashing into a tree at the bottom of the embankment. Moira stood on the brakes and her car skidded to a stop on the shoulder. She raced back as fast as she could. Other cars were stopping and in the distance she could hear sirens. She started down the embankment. Her FBI friend was unconscious, one of his arms was at a funny angle and he was bleeding profusely from several cuts on his face. She heard movement behind her and two EMT men came up to the jeep. They moved her aside and she realized she was shaking violently. She looked around and saw other EMT personal working on the man in the pickup. She had to talk to the police.

Someone she didn't know helped her up the embankment and one of State Police came over to her. She told him she had called 911 and that the truck had run the jeep off the road.

"Don't let that man go!" She said, "He's wanted by the FBI, and the man in the jeep *is* FBI."

It turned out that they had received several 911 calls from people who had seen what was going on, and also one from the FBI ...

130

She waited until her long haired friend was safely in an ambulance on his way to the hospital. The ambulance took off sirens blaring and she asked one of the troopers where they were going. He told her they would be taking him back to Morristown, it was the area trauma center. There was no way she could go back to Philadelphia now. That kid had saved her life and she had to go back and make sure he was all right. She got back in her car and took the next exit to turn around and retrace her steps back north.

Five miles back she saw a large hotel close to an exit and turned off the highway. She drove up to the entrance. The doorman opened the car door and asked if she was staying with them? She was still shaking and hoped she was coherent when she told him that was her intention if they had a room. She popped the trunk. The doorman looked at her with concern as he lifted out Ted's suitcase and wheeled it into the lobby. *Thank God* – a room was available and she booked it then tipped the doorman, who handed her a claim ticket for her car and left.

Once in the room she looked around to find somewhere to hide the suitcase. Not many options. She pushed it to the very back of the closet and covered it with the extra blanket and pillow she found there. The shaking was gradually going away but she badly needed a drink. she kicked off her shoes and raided the refrigerator for a scotch. She thought about the man in the red pick-up truck, thank God he was out of commission.... *Did he have a back-up who had followed her to the hotel? ... Did anyone else know she had the case?...* She prayed nobody knew where she was.

Now that her brain was beginning to function again, it occurred to her that she should have told the State Troopers about the suitcase. Why hadn't she? But then she answered her own question. It had been chaotic; all anyone was thinking about was the accident. She'd told them about the man in the red pickup and the FBI guy in the jeep and the frantic few minutes before the truck had run the jeep off the road, but she had totally forgotten about the suitcase in her trunk. What would have happened if she had told them? They knew nothing about the investigation. It was the FBI and Mike who needed the suitcase. One of the troopers would have put the case in his cruiser and it would

131

have disappeared into some nondescript evidence room. And she *couldn't* lose track of it again. She was glad she hadn't thought to tell them.

 She had had a bad jolt – finally she was realizing just how much danger she was in. And the suitcase was adding to it. It peered out at her from the back of the closet as a constant reminder. She had been so sure of herself that she hadn't listened to Mike when he told her it was dangerous.

She needed to contact him. Damn! He had been right – she should have waited. She felt terrible about the young FBI agent who was in the hospital because of her.

There was no response from Mike. She tried calling the hospital but it was too soon to get any news. She prayed the agent was still alive...

She had dinner in her room and went to bed early but did not sleep well.

SEVENTEEN

Back in England Mike was wrapping up his investigation. He had covered a lot of ground in the past two days. His last interview had been with the commander in charge of the military complex on the Burrows, and it had been a case of good news – bad news. Good news; they had listened to Ted and had followed up on the information he had given the police about three men taking something off a cabin cruiser in the estuary and hiding it in the ruins of the old lighthouse.

"They found it all right." The commander told him. "The man was right to report it. It bloody well was a shoulder mounted rocket launcher. We left it there and waited for them to come back and claim it."

"Did you get them?" Mike asked.

"Only two men came back and absolutely we got them. It just so happened, surprise, surprise, they came back on the day we were carrying out military exercises with live ammunition and practicing bombing runs. The bad guys' intention was to take out one of our planes, but our men got to them first. Nice piece of precision bombing that."

"Did you find out who they were, did you identify the bodies?" Mike asked.

"Not much left to identify I'm afraid." The commander replied.

Bad News, thought Mike. Bang goes another lead...

Later the same day he and Jim were having dinner, pulling together the information they had gathered over the past week to pass it on to the 'Backroom Boys'. They ran down what they had found. The military facility information; the hotel – with the exception of one waiter, everyone thought both Ted and Jill were decidedly strange and paranoid; the bartender at the pub had been run off the road by a blue ford focus; he was able to give Mike a good description of the three men who had visited the pub, and had given the same information to the local Police earlier, and Mike had also visited the George Hotel where the men had stayed. Apart from their physical descriptions, he learnt how long they had stayed, the false identities they had used, and the fact a woman had joined them for part of their stay, but gleaned no other useful information.

Jim had visited all the police stations; the coroner – who he found defensive in the extreme, and the crematorium where he found the woman as defensive as the coroner.

"What a bitch!" He said to Mike.

The phony sister and brother-in-law remained a mystery, but they were most likely the same couple who had followed Jill. More work was needed there…. And why the toothpicks?

As they were finishing up a flurry of emails and texts came in on Mike's phone. He scanned them and exploded.

"Let me guess – the crazy woman, right?" commented Jim.

"The *bloody stupid* crazy woman!" He replied. "Now one of my men is hospitalized and she is fucking lucky to be alive."

He turned to Jim, "I have to get back – can you drive me to Heathrow in time to get the early morning flight out?"

"Of course," Jim replied. "Get your kit together and we'll take off."

EIGHTEEN

Moira woke up gradually. It was Sunday morning and here she was in a hotel room in New Jersey. Everything about yesterday was so unreal she couldn't process it. She turned on the television and found the local news was full of the accident on 287. Graphic video of the red pickup truck crushed into a tree, engine smoking – and the badly damaged black jeep a little way away. She watched as the video showed the EM Technicians putting the two men into separate ambulances, a State trooper climbing into the ambulance with the man from the pickup – and for the first time learnt the name of the young FBI agent – Shawn Peterson. The video caught a glimpse of her in the group of bystanders, standing near one of the officers, hugging herself and visibly upset. She turned the TV off. She didn't need to go back there again. Her phone had been very quiet, no new messages – nothing from Mike, nothing important.

By mid-morning Moira was getting hungry and claustrophobic – she needed to get out. She decided to leave the suitcase in the closet, and put the "Do Not Disturb" sign on the door before pulling it closed behind her. Once in her car she headed north to be closer to the hospital before stopping to eat and bought coffee and a muffin in a Starbucks that she found in the center of Morristown. She took her food outside to a table on the sidewalk facing the Green – joining the local Harley Club taking their Sunday morning constitutional away from their corporate pressures. She pictured them during the week, sans leather,

dressed in their normal business attire.... It was a beautiful day and people were out in force – strolling along the paths that crisscrossed the Green, enjoying the remains of summer. It would soon be over Moira realized. She visualized the Green in the eighteenth century when animals grazed there. It had aged well, no more grazing animals but tall trees and statuary emphasizing the Town's Revolutionary War heritage. Moira was restless. She had tried calling the hospital, but they would not give out any information about Shawn – "Are you a relative?" They had asked. He was able to receive visitors though, so shortly after lunchtime she parked her car in the visitors' garage and went to the reception desk to check in and find his room number. Next stop the gift shop, where she bought some flowers and a card in which she wrote, *Thank you for my life, I'm so sorry you were hurt, it was all my fault. You were magnificent! I can't ever thank you enough.*
Get better fast!
Moira

Shawn was asleep when she entered his room and looked awful. Part of his head had been shaved, he had a black eye and numerous cuts and deep purple bruises – an I.V dripped into the only arm visible above the covers.

He opened one eye and saw her,

"Hey." He mumbled. "How you doin'?"

She poured out her thanks – She knew she owed him her life and would never be able to thank him enough. It would have been her at the bottom of the embankment if it hadn't been for him protecting her. She felt incredibly guilty for him getting hurt. She knew it was her fault. She should have listened to Mike... Could she get him anything? Was he going to be all right? ... She knew she was babbling on but couldn't stop. Shawn closed his eyes again.

"I'm going to be OK." He said, "Couple of days and I'll be back on the race track."

Footsteps could be heard coming down the corridor and Mike came into the room. He was startled to see Moira, but pointedly ignored her and went straight to Shawn.

"Great job, Man." He said. "You saved that stupid woman's life."

136

Off on the side Moira felt her temper flaring.

"Don't be hard on her Mike, she feels bad enough already." Shawn said wearily, eyes closed again. "She's already said she's sorry."

"I hope she thanked you for saving her life." Mike was still furious...

Shawn nodded carefully, "First thing she said." Eyes closed.

He was drifting off to sleep.

Moira put the flowers and her card on his bedside cabinet and quietly left the room.

Mike patted Shawn's shoulder. "I'll be back tomorrow."

He caught up with her and exploded.

"Does it ever occur to you to listen to anyone other than yourself? All I can say is if you can only hear your own voice, then you'd better start analyzing the possible ramifications of your decisions before you act on them."

Moira was trying to keep her temper under control.

"I've said I'm sorry, I've admitted you were right, I should have waited, I feel guilty as hell about Shawn getting hurt, but please don't call me stupid in front of other people! If that's your opinion, fine, but that's between you and me...And just for your information I am *not* stupid!"

He broke in, "You're so bloody single-minded it makes you stupid! You only listen to yourself. Take the time to listen to other people occasionally, you've no idea how much you would benefit from it!"

They lapsed into silence, both still furious, walking together only because they were leaving the hospital at the same time.

In the lobby Moira drew ahead and entered the automatic revolving door first. He let her go ahead and followed in the next section. On the way to the parking garage he caught up with her again.

"Is Ted's bag in your trunk?"

"No, it's in my room at the hotel."

"I'll follow you back and take it off your hands."

"Good!" She said. "And you can take that damn tracking device off my car at the same time."

Mike did not answer. He grinned to himself. *Good old Shawn he thought....*

Back at the hotel Mike accompanied her to her room and she pulled the case out from the back of the closet. A new thought occurred to her that if she stayed another night not only would she be wearing the same clothes for yet another day but also she would leave without any luggage......

"Do you mind waiting while I call the desk and let them know I'm leaving? Then we can leave together with the luggage I arrived with." She said sarcastically, still angry.

In response Mike put the case on the desk and started to go through it while he waited. Dan had taken the business papers out when he first got it back to his office. *Mike made a mental note to interview him as soon as he was back from China.* At first glance the only contents were clothes and one paperback travel book on North Devon.

While he waited for Moira to get off the phone he picked up the book and flipped through the pages finding nothing unusual, no notes, nothing. Then he held the book upside down by the covers and shook it, bending it backwards hoping to see something fall out. Again, nothing. He threw it back in the suitcase. After his rough handling the stiff paper covers curled away from the rest of the pages and the spine had become concave. He picked it up again and examined it more carefully. Bending back the covers had caused a vertical crease almost to the bottom of the spine. *That's curious he thought, why isn't that last section creased?* He looked more carefully and ran his fingers down the spine to where the crease ended and felt a small stiff square. *Clever Ted! He thought....* At the bottom of the book Ted had very carefully loosened the cover from the back of the pages and had managed to insert the micro SD from his cell phone up into the spine.

"Damn!" He said out loud.

Moira was on hold and looked up startled by the excitement in his voice.

"What?" She asked.

He told her quickly that he had found the SD drive from Ted's phone pushed up into the spine of the travel book.

"You nearly ready?" He asked. "I've got to get this back to the lab. Come on, let's go!"

God he's like a teenager she thought as the Front Desk came back on the line and told her she was all set.

They left together, Mike wheeling the case. His mood had radically changed after his find.

"Sorry I yelled at you earlier, it was unprofessional." He said.

Then over his shoulder as he hurried to his car.

"But it was a bloody stupid thing you did."

She opened her mouth to answer him but then thought better of it – besides, he was half way across the parking lot by then.

NINETEEN

A week later, in a small non-descript courtroom, a police officer was giving testimony.

The police had viewed the CCTV cameras at the entrances to the bridge and had canvased all the cars that used the bridge in either direction between Thursday night and Friday morning. Only one person thought he might have witnessed something.

The man was called to the stand. He had been driving east on the bridge going home after an evening with friends in Staten Island. He gave his address in Brooklyn. He had seen a woman running along the side of the bridge on the opposite side. He had not seen her get out of a car but there were several cars travelling in the same direction at the time. One of them close to her was going slowly. He thought maybe the people in the car were checking on her. It was *possible* that a man *might* have got out and gone after her, but he couldn't swear to it. He might have imagined it. He assumed that she'd had a row with a boyfriend or was drunk and was trying to get home to Staten Island. She didn't look as if she was going to climb over the railings, she was in a hurry. By then he had gone by her and was watching everything in his rearview mirror, and in a very short time he had travelled on too far to see anything else. His assumption was that a car had picked her up or she'd continued along the bridge on foot……

Then it was Moira's turn. In the end she was on the stand very briefly. She was asked about her friendship with Jill, but was cut off when she vehemently stated that Jill was not a fragile personality, nor was she paranoid, and she was the least likely person to take her own life. "She would have been determined to discover why Ted had been killed. She would never have given up."

She pointed to the letter from Jill, and asked why no one would believe her – Jill Davis was not a stupid person and would not have imagined she was being followed......

The police officer was briefly called back to the stand.

"Yes, the department had been in touch with their British counterparts who had reiterated the conclusion of their investigation into the death of Edward Barnes – that the probable cause of death was that he had taken his own life. They had noted that in the area it had happened the edge of the cliff was flat and solid, and there were no indications of skid marks which would have been visible if he had slipped. In addition, there were reports of paranoiac behavior. Miss Davis had arrived three days after his body had been found and had been very upset and adamant that he had not killed himself. Regarding the letter Miss Davis had sent to Miss Gregory. There was no additional information in it. Miss Davis had not personally witnessed any of the events, the letter was hearsay."

The coroner started to sum up. He went through all the evidence that had been presented, taking into consideration the extensive investigation the police had carried out after Jill's body was identified. Lastly, he turned to Moira.

"Unfortunately you are the only one who thinks there was foul play and that she was thrown off the bridge. The investigation by the British authorities found that Miss Davis was very upset after her friend's death and incidences of unbalanced and paranoiac behavior were reported by several people. I'm afraid you are alone in your belief that she and her friend Edward Barnes met violent deaths at the hands of unknown persons. No one will believe you that Miss Davis did not throw herself off the bridge."

He faced forward and gave his verdict.

"It is the opinion of this inquest that Jillian Davis threw herself from the Verrazano Narrows Bridge while the balance of her mind was disturbed following the probable suicide of her friend Edward Barnes while on vacation in England."

Moira was furious. She couldn't believe what had happened. The coroner had already left the room and the few spectators were beginning to file out. She wondered why they had come. Friends of the family or just people with a morbid curiosity? She wondered if one of them might be FBI keeping an eye on things – *or please not – maybe a friend of the man who had been stalking her?* The room was almost empty, only four people still sitting on one of the benches, one a woman being comforted by one of the men. She realized it was Tom and Joan – the other two were probably Joan's sister and her husband Moira thought. She had been so caught up with her own role in the drama of the inquest she had not noticed before that they were there. She went over to them.
"I'm so sorry about the verdict. It was so wrong! I know Jill didn't kill herself. I'm so sorry they wouldn't believe me."
They were all visibly shaken by the verdict, it was not the time to linger over social niceties and she left them, so angry about the stupidity of the verdict she could hardly see where she was walking.

She was almost to the exit when a man reached out and grasped her arm.
"Hey!" he said.
She turned and recognized Dan Murphy, his face a stony mask.
"You're supposed to be in China."
She was surprised to see him but his presence was comforting. She remembered how she had been struck by his air of confidence the one and only time they had met. Now his sudden appearance steadied her, and she managed to get her anger under control. But she saw that he too was furious.
"I got back late last night I wanted to make the inquest." Then he exploded. "Christ, how wrong can they be! Jill would never have killed herself, and the verdict is so final – it makes me fucking mad. First Ted and now Jill."
He looked at her and his expression softened slightly,

142

"Come on," he said, "I'll buy you dinner. Let's get out of here."

They had a long, long dinner, both were wound up about the verdict and how the inquest dismissed the information in many of the statements, including Moira's. They kept returning to the same subject. Moira could not let it go.

"They were so bloody stupid no one listened to what I said. Nobody believed me." She was frustrated and disgusted.

Dan's anger was more controlled but just as deep.

"Ted and Jill were not the type to kill themselves – how could the coroner believe that? I don't see how he could possibly have got it so wrong!"

They both vented about the verdict through their first drink then gradually moved on to what had happened while Dan was in China through a refill. During the appetizers Dan spoke about his China trip and then they drifted back to Ted and Jill again with another drink, while they waited for their entrées. Their meals eventually arrived, but by that time their conversation had turned personal.

"You know I met Holly." Moira said.

"Did you." He grimaced.

"She didn't know about Ted and Jill and was very upset when she heard – she couldn't stop talking about it... "

"And about our breakup too I'll bet."

"I didn't want her to start in about that, so I changed the subject." She replied.

"Well I'll tell you what happened...." From Dan.

"I don't want to hear about it from you either. I don't like carrying other people's baggage around." Moira retorted.

"I'm going to talk about it this one time." Dan said. "I want you to know. I know Holly's upset, but she's impossible, we never should have got married, she should go back to Michigan. We met in college and had the perfect romance and the perfect wedding. Unfortunately, her idea of the perfect life and mine turned out to be totally different. We were married for seven imperfect years. We had nothing in common, Ted and Jill were the only people we could call mutual friends, and even they gave up on us.... She hated it here, we bickered all the time. It was destroying us both and I couldn't take it anymore. The sad thing is I don't have any good feeling left about her anymore. I'm just so thankful she's out of my life."

"Wow!" said Moira, who by then was starting to feel the effects of the wine they had been drinking, "That's quite a confession!"

He didn't smile.

"I 'm glad I told you." He said. "I'm glad I got it of my chest – and I'm sorry if I've burdened you." Finally he smiled. "OK your turn, burden me."

"There's not much to tell," she replied. "A couple of long relationships, one finished badly, one I moved away and the long distance thing just didn't work and it petered out. Several shorter flings – I tend to be very leery about committing – probably too careful."

That was all she was prepared to say. She drank some more of her wine. "This is getting depressing." She said.

"Drink up, I'll get another bottle." He signaled the waiter.

As they left the restaurant at the end of the evening Dan looked at Moira, "There's no way you're going back to Philadelphia tonight, come on, you can sleep on my sofa." He said. And hailed a cab.

Moira woke up next morning with a crashing headache. She opened her eyes slowly and looked up at a strange ceiling *Christ she felt awful....* Dan turned over in his sleep and threw his arm over her. *Hell! She wasn't ready for this...* Very carefully she slid out from under his arm and went to the bathroom gathering up her clothes on the way. She sat on the commode, her head swimming, leant back and closed her eyes. She longed to go back to sleep. She felt terrible.

Presently she opened her eyes again and carefully looked around. A half used tube of toothpaste sat on the edge of the basin, she squeezed some onto her finger and rubbed it over her teeth. It didn't help much. She turned on the shower and thanked God for the water drenching her body. She caught the spray in her mouth, rinsed and spat it out. She was coming back to life...very .... slowly.... She turned off the shower, dried herself on the only towel she could find, and dressed. Then quietly opened the bathroom door.

Dan appeared to still be asleep. *Damn! They had both drunk so much last night!* She wondered if he felt as bad as she did. She explored his apartment and found the tiny space he called his kitchen. The shower was running again – Dan was awake. She found the coffee pods in one of the cabinets and started to make coffee for them both.

The shower stopped abruptly and soon after he came up behind her wearing a robe and put his arms around her.

"God, we drank a lot last night." He said nuzzling her neck, his head heavy on her shoulder.

And she knew he was feeling as bad as she was.

She handed him a coffee and moved away. He looked at her quizzically.

"I've got to get back to Philly, I'm sorry Dan, I didn't mean for this to happen."

"I don't think either of us did." He replied. "Listen, we both feel like shit, can we talk about this some other time?"

She was thankful for the suggestion. She picked up her bag and he followed her to the door.

"Do you mind if I don't come down? The doorman will get you a cab." He kissed her carefully then groaned.

"I need some more sleep. I'm going back to bed. Will you be O.K?"

She said she would be and that she planned to do exactly the same as soon as she was home.

He closed the door behind her and headed back to bed, his head worse than ever. He needed sleep. He felt bad that she had left like that... *I should have taken her down to the lobby and made sure she'd got a cab...* He had known she would be at the inquest but he had arrived late, and it was not until everything was over and he was about to leave, that he'd caught sight of her coming up the stairs to the exit, *so angry she could hardly see where she was going.* He was glad that he had been there for her... *She was pretty damn vulnerable underneath that tough exterior...* He would like to get to know her better but last night had probably screwed that up too. Damn! this was not right! So many bad things had happened. His thoughts returned to yesterday and the verdict, and his anger surged back. Ted, Jill, Holly. What next? *So much chaos....* So much to figure out, so much to get resolved.

The speeding train rolled Moira's thoughts into one giant ball that filled her brain. She leant back in her seat and closed her eyes. Too many jumbled thoughts. She wished last night hadn't happened like that... *Too much drink... too many emotions... Poor Jill... Poor Ted... Dan. Nothing made sense... She couldn't think straight... She had to clear her head... She needed sleep...*

TWENTY

Dan called several days later apologizing for not calling before –
Continual meetings catching up on work and then a meeting with the
FBI guy Mike Balmer had taken up every free moment and he had
wanted to have the time to talk without interruptions.

She was glad that he hadn't called sooner, she was still trying to process
their last meeting.

He started right in.

"Look." He said. "Both of us are terribly upset about Ted and Jill, we're
still trying to make sense of it all, without much success, and the verdict
was the final straw. It was good to be with you because you knew Jill
and had met Ted. I know for me it was very good to be able to talk
about it. And yes, we drank much too much but I don't regret what
happened one bit, I hope you don't either?"

Moira agreed that it had been a great help to be able to vent – and she
agreed that they had drunk too much and, no, she didn't regret what
happened.

"Are you free for dinner this weekend? I can come down to Philly...."

"You see that's the problem, she said. "It's like we're continuing Jill and
Teds' relationship, channeling their lives Do you understand what I'm
trying to say?"

Her rejection threw him. He wanted to see her again, and had thought
she would want to see him too. Objectively he could see what was
bothering her – though he didn't think she was right – last night he had

147

thought they had connected on a deeper level than just the bond they had commiserating about Ted and Jill. Had he been wrong?

"Personally I think we are both strong enough individuals to be able to separate ourselves from Ted and Jill – but they are our common background and we can't get away from that."

Quietly Moira answered.

"I just need some space to sort things out. I don't want to get to know you in a cocoon with Ted and Jill there too…"

"I understand what you're saying," he replied. "I think you're wrong, but I understand – so no dinner this weekend."

Then he couldn't resist adding. "Although personally I think it would be easier for both of us to get through their senseless deaths with each other's help. I'm not going away. I hope we can stay in touch?"

"I'd like that." She said.

Part of her already wondering if she had made the correct decision, part of her beginning to realize how much she was going to miss his support.

Life gradually settled back to normal – except that it didn't.

Nobody knew if the FBI was any closer to finding out what had happened. They were told that "things were moving quickly" – except to those involved it felt that the ball had been dropped, they were lost in a fog and no one seemed to think that they were important enough to be included in the loop. Moira found herself watching people closely and several times got out of an elevator when a strange man got in after her, even if there were other people in the elevator. She hated this new suspicious self. She hated feeling so vulnerable.

And then there was Mike Balmer. He called Moira shortly after the inquest. He knew she must be furious at the verdict and he wanted to know if she was all right. Again, he reassured her that the investigation was going well…. And then he added he was going to be in Philadelphia in a few days and felt he owed her a dinner. She accepted, hoping she would learn more about the progress they were making with the investigation if she saw him face to face.

He had a second important reason for them to get together which he didn't mention on the phone, but he kept the call going, and threw her a few crumbs of new information. One of the keys from Jill's condo was to Ted's apartment but when his team got there it had been ransacked and they had found nothing of interest. They found nothing else in Ted's suitcase. The micro SD drive in the travel book had turned out to be the prize piece of information. On it were daily notes from Ted, including places and descriptions, and he had also managed to surreptitiously photograph the three men in the pub, and the man and woman who were putting flowers on a grave while he was placing the third toothpick, who he thought were the same couple who had been at the chapel when he had placed the second toothpick earlier. That was all definitely helping their investigation....

Mike added that he was sure she would like to know that Shawn was doing well and was now in Rehab, and would be fine.

Moira asked about the man in the pickup truck and Mike said he was alive but it was still touch and go if he would make it. In one of his conscious moments he had told them that he had been approached in a bar by a man who paid him to follow her when she went to get the case and take it from her. *But Mike did not share with her that the man had also been paid to "take her out." That worried him...* It was the main reason he had called her.

Several days later they met at a downtown restaurant. He was there before her and stood up as the host guided her to his table and seated her opposite him.

He grinned at her a trifle sheepishly.

"It's good to see you again, I'm glad you said you would come."

She stopped herself making a snide remark about their last angry meeting – just commenting at her surprise when he called.

"Ah, I have a big heart, I like to give people a second chance." He joked, then seeing the sudden flash of anger in her eyes realized that his attempt at humor was ill-timed.

"Seriously." He said. "I'm truly sorry that I blew up at you, it was really un-called for, Can you accept my apology? It truly is sincere."

Finally she smiled.

"We were both pretty angry, I wasn't particularly nice either. Let's forget it. It's good to see you too."

"One more piece of business and then we'll enjoy our dinner."

He slid a phone across the table to her.

"This is another reason I wanted to get together. Your phone was hacked. That's how they found out you going to pick up Ted's case. I bet you don't even have a password on it, do you? Here's a new one. It's encrypted. This is the only one you use to contact me or if you want to share your thoughts with anyone else."

She felt guilty all over again...

Then as usual, he changed the subject and the atmosphere of the conversation, apologizing yet again for balling her out, adding it had given him a kick the way she had fired back at him.

"I like a woman who can stand up for herself." He said with a grin.

"You made me angry." She said.

But she was enjoying the dinner. *Mike could be very entertaining when he wanted to be she thought...* But then, she'd figured that out already...

At the end of the evening he accompanied her up to her apartment but would not come in.

"I have to get going." He said. "I'll call you next time I'm in town?"

He gave her a chaste kiss and left for the elevator without waiting for her answer.

"Goodnight, thank you for dinner." She called after him.

He turned at the elevator door and waved.

"See you soon."

And he was off...

It was the start of a very strange period in Moira's life. Mike began to embark on an old fashioned wooing. He would text her often and started to show up in Philadelphia on a regular basis, giving increasingly feeble excuses. Flowers showed up at her workplace after they went to bed for the first time. She didn't know how to process it all, but it helped to balance the horrible, complicated emotions she was trying to assimilate, and it made her feel safe to have to have him there. He was fun, and entertaining, and attentive, and probably just what she needed... on a short term basis....

And what of Mike? He struggled to find a good reason to be with her while the investigation was on-going. From a professional point of view he knew he was skating on thin ice – he gave himself the excuse that he was tracking down the men who were stalking her, moving the investigation forward – but she intrigued him and he liked to be with her – that was the main reason...

Meanwhile Dan had begun interviewing candidates to fill Ted's position. He was finding it difficult and knew he was being extra critical of them, comparing them all to his friend. In addition, after the inquest the media had picked up on the story of Jill's "suicide" – and especially on Moira's insistence that both Ted and Jill had been murdered. It didn't help. Most of the candidates referred to Ted's death in passing, offering their condolences, but one candidate appeared to be overly concerned about what had happened. Interspersed with his other questions he delved into Ted's death and kept returning to the same subject – *Did the company think he had got caught up in something in England? ... Should he be concerned about a carryover danger to the new hire? Was the work Ted had been doing dangerous? If he was hired, was there anything he should know about what happened on his UK trip? Had they been told anything about the reason he was killed? Did they know what he had got involved with?* The man was pleasant, and his qualifications were adequate, but the reason he stood out was his almost obsessive interest in Ted's death. Scattered throughout the interview the questions were a subtle undercurrent and it took Dan a while to put his finger on it, but once he did it stuck out like a sore thumb. Why the obsessive interest in Ted, when he should have been focused on the company and the responsibilities of the position?

The first interviews were over. The applicants knew the drill – only some of them would be called back for the second round.

Dan sat at his desk and thought about the man who was so interested in Ted – it had raised his hackles, *maybe the man was just weird*. But the more he thought about it the more suspicious he became. He contacted Mike.

Mike got back to him fast asking many questions and then asking him to keep the man's application and anything he might have touched for DNA testing; someone would pick them up later that day.

He was a good as his word and a messenger collected the carefully packaged items before the office closed for the night.

Several days later Mike showed up.

"You were right to contact us." He said. "The man is on one of the watch lists."

Dan leant back in his chair. He had not expected that. In fact, he had felt foolish contacting Mike.

Mike paused to let his words sink in.

"What I would like you to do is call him back for a second interview. We will set it up before hand – you may not see us but we will be there. Also." He said, "I would like you to agree to wear a wire, it would be very helpful to record his conversation."

Dan agreed. "Of course, anything to get to the bottom of this."

"I have to warn you, this is not a nice man…" Mike added. "You have every right not to agree to my request."

"No I'll do it." Dan answered.

Everything was ready when ten days later the man checked in at the front desk for his second interview. The fifth floor receptionist was notified and a few minutes later she appeared from one of the elevators and escorted him up to Dan's office. She orchestrated the comings and goings of all of the fifth floor, monitoring them from her desk that faced the elevator. From there nothing and no one got passed her. She enjoyed her work – it suited her to a tee. She wondered if the man she has just brought up from the lobby would be Ted's replacement. He seemed nice enough, but she still could not get over what had happened to Ted.

Dan was waiting in his office. He was tense. He still wondered why the man had applied for the position – the only reason he could think of was that he wanted to find out what the company knew about Ted's death. Did the man have any clue that the FBI was involved? He hoped not. He was very conscious of the wire taped to his torso and had prepared for the interview well in advance. His plan was to stretch it out as long as he possible, hoping the FBI would be able to glean some useful new information from the man's remarks. Mike's words that *"This is not a nice man"* kept bouncing around inside his head. *He had to be careful not to raise any red flags. The last thing he wanted was to make the man suspicious that he was about to walk into a trap* ….

The receptionist knocked on his open door, introduced the candidate and left, closing the door behind her.

Dan rose from his chair and reached across his desk to shake hands, inviting the man to sit in the chair opposite him. The usual pleasantries, then the interview began. Detailed questions about the man's past work experiences; his education; how he would approach the position he was applying for, and what he could bring to the position, kept their conversation going. Finally, he asked for references. By then it was close to lunchtime and Dan asked him to join him so they could continue talking –

"There's a good deli just down the street."

They left his office and stopped at the receptionist's desk for his visitor to sign out before they left the floor.

Half way across the main lobby his phone rang. It was the receptionist telling him that his visitor had forgotten his briefcase – he'd left it by her desk. He turned to the man to pass on the information and saw the man pulling his phone out of his pocket.

"That reminds me." He said. "I have to make a call."

Suddenly there was enormous activity around them. Three men rushed his companion, one knocking the phone from his hand, the other two pinning him to the floor and handcuffing his hands behind his back. At the same time four more men rushed towards the elevator and up the stairs. Someone yelled to security,

"Clear the building!"

Suddenly Mike was there directing operations, too involved with sealing the area and hustling the man into a van to acknowledge Dan. The bomb squad appeared as if by magic and rushed upstairs. It was chaos. It seemed like an eternity but probably less than ten minutes before everyone was milling around outside. Dan leant back against the building, eyes closed, still sweating. The receptionist came up to him shaking.

"You all right?" He asked, putting his arm around her shoulders. "Thank God you noticed that bag and called me." *She's more than made up for giving Holly Ted's case, he thought to himself...*

Mike came over and beckoned for Dan to follow him.

"Thank you! Sincerely." He said. "FYI it was a bomb, and it's been diffused. They're going to let everyone back in."

"Christ! A bomb! I never expected that. Can you tell me what the hell's going on?" Dan asked.

"Not yet," Mike replied. "But we're getting there. This was a giant leap forward today. Thank God you were wearing that wire and we heard the call from the receptionist. Narrow squeak that! Come on, I'll get that wire off you."

Privately Mike was still trying to connect all the dots. Planting the bomb had come out of left field. Another facet, another piece to fit into the puzzle. He knew there was a definite connection between the organization in Devon and the group who were operating in the States. He figured the man had probably applied for Ted's old position to discover what the company knew, but why the bomb? This was the first time the group had used explosives. It was a hell of a way to make a statement if that was all it was.... a very dangerous 'in your face move'. What were they trying to prove?

Hours later Dan was back in his apartment. He was a confident man – people were drawn to him for just that reason - but the day's events had shaken him to the core and temporarily knocked his legs from under him. It had been completely out of his control. He was exhausted. He poured himself a stiff drink then put his feet up on the sofa and turned on the game. He needed a diversion.

He thought about Moira and wished she was with him. *She should know what happened today.*

He reached for his phone and scrolled through his contacts to call her. He wanted to hear her voice.

They talked for half an hour and he told her about his day. She was alarmed when she heard about the bomb and how close he had been to the danger. The fact that it had turned out well didn't lessen her concern. The bomb raised her anxiety to a whole new level.

Dan tried to relieve her fears,

'You shouldn't worry, Mike had it under control," he said, trying to reassure her. "He goes through this sort of thing every day."

"You're different from Mike," she said. "That's his job – besides, he's an adrenaline junkie."

Dan picked up something in her voice.

"Have you seen Mike recently?"

"We've had dinner once or twice when he's been in town." She lied.

TWENTY-ONE

Early Fall Joan and Tom sent out invitations to Jill's memorial service. It was to be held in one of the historic old churches close to the University and they hoped everyone would be able to come for a celebration of Jill's life.

Dan called Moira the next day asking if she was going. Yes, she was, it was not until the week after next but she had made sure that she would be in town.

"If I take the train down can you pick me up from the station?" He asked.

"I'd be happy to, I'm glad you're planning on going." She answered.

God! We're being so formal with each other....

"Thanks, I'll look up the train times and let you know when I'll be arriving. It will be good to see you again."

They exchanged pleasantries for a while, finally starting to relax with each other before the call ended.

The two weeks had flown by. Summer was well and truly over and although the weather was still fairly warm, the mornings were crisp and the daylight hours were getting shorter. *In a couple of weeks, the clocks go back* Moira mused as she drove to Jill's memorial service. It was a beautiful fall day and the trees around Princeton were putting on a brilliant display. In places they formed a yellow canopy over the road casting a golden glow on everything. She would have been happy if I weren't for the sad reason she was going to Princeton. Random thoughts ran through her head as she drove … *Call it a celebration of life as much as you want but the sad truth is that a beautiful alive person has been senselessly killed …… Someone who still had so much more life to live.* It made her very angry, and very sad…

She reached Princeton and found her way to the station in plenty of time for Dan's train. A few minutes later it pulled in to the station and she watched his tall figure jump out of a carriage and come swinging down the platform towards her. He put his arms around her and gave her a lingering kiss and she felt herself automatically pull back slightly, not wanting to let him think she had changed her mind about their relationship. He looked into her face and smiled,

"All right, I get it, I won't push, but it is good to see you." He said.

They drove to the church and found parking. It was a short walk and they were almost there when Moira saw Mike standing by the entrance... *Damn! this is going to be awkward she thought.* He greeted them at the door – a model of decorum, shaking Dan's hand warmly and grinning at Moira.

"I found I could get away." He said to them both. "We'd better go in." He put his hand in the small of Moira's back to guide her in and the familiarity of the move set off warning bells in Dan's head. He stiffened visibly. *Damn! Thought Moira for the second time in as many minutes, I didn't want this to happen...* They sat together not far from the front, Dan remote and quietly seething on one side, Mike relaxed and taking in everything on the other, and Moira in the middle trying to orchestrate an awkward situation.

The service over, everyone adjourned to a reception next door. The three of them walked over together to talk to Joan and Tom. Moira found them much changed since their first meeting. They looked older, and moved more slowly, she was so sad for them. She hugged Joan and hoped she was O.K. *She did not know what else to say...* Tom came and joined their conversation. They were glad to see her and thanked her for coming. She stayed talking to them, about Jill, and Ted, and their hope that the FBI would solve the crime and round up everyone involved very soon. They were grateful that at least the FBI did not think that Jill killed herself. That had helped.

157

Dan and Mike had wandered off, talking about the latest advances in the investigation. Talking about Ted and Jill…. Dan suddenly stopped walking and wheeled to face Mike.

"Be careful with Moira," he said vehemently. "Don't hurt her!"

Mike was surprised at his anger.

"She's a big girl," he said confidently. "She can look after herself."

"She's more fragile than you know – she's going through a rough time right now."

"She knows what she's doing, don't worry, she'll be fine."

Dan turned on his heel and walked away. Mike's cavalier attitude had made him even angrier. He had to get out of there. He went over to Tom and Joan to say goodbye, then realized Moira was there, still talking with them.

"I'm leaving." He said, addressing Moira, "I'll walk to the station."

"Wait! I'll take you." She called after him.

"I need the exercise." He replied, raising his arm to wave goodbye without turning around.

"But I want to take you, please?"

Grudgingly he stopped walking and waited for her as she said goodbye to Joan and Tom before following him out.

They were silent most of the way to the station.

"You lied to me." He said finally.

She didn't reply.

Several minutes later she spoke again.

"He's fun to be with and I need that just now. He's a good guy."

"He's good at his job I'll give you that." Dan was still angry. "But I wouldn't trust him for one minute with women. You're going to get hurt. He'll be off as soon as the newness wears off. He enjoys a challenge that one, and once the conquest's over, poof! He'll be gone!"

"I'm not looking for long term." She said.

"And," he went on, "I thought you didn't want to be with someone who reminded you of Ted and Jill the whole time – Christ, what do you think this guy's doing – Chasing the bad guys who killed Ted and Jill, that's all…"

"I enjoy his company – and I feel safe when he's around." She added quietly.

"I guess having the whole FBI behind him might be a factor." Dan said sarcastically.

They sat in the car lapsed into silence, waiting...The train arrived and he opened the door and got out.

"Stay in touch." He said without much enthusiasm.

He walked away across the platform and got on the train.

Moira started her car and drove out of the station. She hadn't wanted Dan to find out about Mike like that. She hadn't wanted to hurt him and she was afraid she had. She was furious with Mike for turning up without letting her know he was coming, she could have paved the way if she had known he was going to be there. Then she remembered Dan's recent words.... *He planned this, she thought. It's all part of the conquest....*

She spent the afternoon driving around country roads, the brilliant fall colors gradually soothing her anger. When she finally got back to her building Mike was there, sitting in the lobby as she figured he would be. She hoped he'd been waiting for hours. She walked past him into the elevator and he followed her.

Her anger came back.

"You bastard!" She said. "Why didn't you tell me you were coming?"

"Oh, what difference would it have made... Dan would still have been upset. He had to know sometime." He was not contrite.

"You planned this!" She said with the sudden realization. "This wasn't about Dan. You showed up this afternoon so everyone would know that you and I were together – that I'd chosen you over Dan. You wanted me to acknowledge publicly, that you had 'won' me ... Dan just happened to be collateral damage."

They had reached her apartment door. "Just go away – you really are a bastard – it was me you were manipulating and I don't like it!"

It crossed Mike's mind that this fight was serious and could bring their relationship crashing down. He did not want that to happen. They both had short fuses, and had fought before, but this time it felt different ......

Moira reached in her bag and found her keys. He took them from her and opened the door, then followed her in and kicked the door shut behind him. He leant back against it and pulled her to him, his arms around her body, holding her to him. She pushed her hands against his shoulders trying to loosen his grip. It didn't work and he kept her close, his fingers spread out, pressing against her spine .... *God, she's exciting he thought!* ..... He knew she was very angry but he knew he was good at calming her and hoped he could soothe her anger again this time. He wanted her to forgive him, and he wanted to be with her.

He buried his head in her neck and kissed her, planting soft light kisses all over her neck and throat.

Against her will she could feel her anger starting to ebb, and hated the way he could always diffuse her temper.

"I'm sorry." He said, trying to sound humble.

"No you're not." She said.

He looked up from her neck and grinned.

"Well, maybe a tiny bit."

She wasn't going to let him off that easily. "Dan was right. It's all about the conquest with you."

"I do like to win." He said with a mischievous grin and planted a deep lingering kiss on her lips.

As usual it worked, her anger had gone – and it was only later that she recognized she had let him manipulate her once again...

TWENTY-TWO

Halloween came and went, the clocks fell back an hour and the weather got colder. The nights closed in. As usual the first early snowstorm took everyone by surprise. Then suddenly November was almost over. There seemed to be little progress in bringing down the network that had killed Ted and Jill. They all had finally had to come to grips with the fact that Ted and Jill were not the focus but only a minor piece of what had become a much larger investigation – though they knew the FBI were still actively trying to find their killers, that was some solace.
As far as anyone knew the case was still wide open. So the people responsible were still out here. There was still the fear of being stalked, or worse, a bomb being set off in a crowded place. To Mike this was very normal and he could be objective about the pace of the investigation, but to Joan, Tom, Dan and Moira it made life very difficult. It was an added burden. The frustration of the unknown added to their grief and their loss. It was a very hard time.

Mike was in Philadelphia chasing down some lead and as he had for the past three months, he called Moira. She puzzled him, he really liked her but he didn't like it when she invaded his thoughts. He knew that if he had to choose between any long term commitment and his work, it would be no contest, there wasn't room in his life for both and his work would win out hands down. He was not self-analytical, he had stumbled upon a lifestyle that suited him to a tee and it did not occur to him to

161

analyze why it worked so well, it might threaten his effectiveness. He got to her apartment around six, and settled down on her sofa with a drink, watching her get ready to go out.

Moira had had a busy day with several meetings which had gone on interminably. She was glad that Mike had called – even if it was only ten minutes before he showed up at her door –the excitement of him appearing out of the blue was beginning to wear thin – and seeing him on the sofa, already with a drink in hand, she was starting to worry about how much he drank when he was "Off the clock," as he called it. They were very different people. He was terrific fun to be with but totally unreliable, shooting off to parts unknown without any warning. She realized his work was an escape hatch for him.

Not knowing that he would be in town she had planned to go to a reception at an art gallery downtown, and now Mike tagged along. It was not one of his usual habitats – unless someone had heisted some artwork he would not have thought to visit a gallery, but for Moira he tried to appear interested and enthusiastic. She watched him circling the room, wine glass in hand, engaging in conversation with everyone, glancing occasionally at the art…. She knew he was bored and they did not stay there as long as Moira would have if she had been there by herself.

At dinner Moira broached the subject "I'm going to my Georgetown friends for Thanksgiving. Want to join me if you're free?"

"I'd love to." He said – then added in a thick Irish brogue, "Just remember me name's John Flaherty."

She laughed. "You should take up acting when you leave the FBI."

"I'll never leave! I'd probably be dead from the drink before the year was over. Look at my body, I'd go to fat in a heartbeat – excuse the pun – no control for the drink…."

"It doesn't seem to affect your work." She said.

He got serious, "Ah, that's my salvation – I need the structure – it's probably the reason I love my work so, it gives me the highs at the same time it curbs the drink. But hey my girl, you aren't exactly a teetotaler are you?"

"No, but I know when to stop."

He grinned, "Smart woman."

The atmosphere suddenly changed and they looked at each other across the table with the same sudden realization.

They automatically reached out and joined hands.

"It's over, isn't it?"

"I think it is."

"Will we still be friends?"

"You'll probably hear from me every now and then."

"What happens if you die?"

He laughed out loud breaking the tension and she joined in.

"I'll make sure you're notified." He promised.

Their coffee arrived and they finished their meal without much conversation.

"Come on, I'll get you home." He said.

He parked the car outside her apartment and leant over to kiss her, then met her eyes.

"One for the road?" He asked.

She grinned.

"Why not." She said.

And they went up to her apartment together.

TWENTY-THREE

Early December Moira was sitting at her desk, figuring out her travel schedule for the first quarter of the New Year. It was coming up fast. She missed the excitement of Mike showing up on a moment's notice, but she was glad it was finished. She was not into letting a good thing deteriorate once the writing was on the wall. Then she thought about Dan. She missed him too – something had happened at the memorial service for Jill, something more than just him seeing her with Mike, but she didn't know what. He had been distant ever since. They emailed occasionally but it was not the same. He was so different from Mike. He would want a lot more from her if they ever got into a relationship – although that seemed very unlikely at this point. They had started out with too much baggage and it had only got worse – And then there was his recent divorce... Still a lot of negative energy floating around there! *So you've blown off two men who you really like in the past two months.... What is wrong with you?* Moira was beginning to wonder if she was that afraid of commitment, could she really be that immature? She remembered her words to Dan during their drunken dinner, that she'd had more flings than long-term relationships...

She got back to her calendar. Maybe she should be thinking about some New Year resolutions too.

But first there was Christmas and she was going home to visit her parents in Canada. A package arrived just before she left. Inside she found a bright red scarf and a note: *Merry Christmas! Now that you*

don't have me you're going to need this to keep you warm in Canada.
Love Mike.
She grinned and packed the scarf in her case, wondering vaguely what
both he and Dan were going to be doing for the holidays.

 It was good to be home and see her parents and her brother Alistair –
who had managed to make it home as well this year with a new
girlfriend in tow. The family would have their traditional Christmas with
all the trimmings, chestnuts in the open fireplace and long hikes to walk
off their meals. She was happy to be home. The girlfriend was from
Florida and did not like the cold weather but soldiered on when they
went skating and on a trip to show her Niagara Falls on a bitterly cold
day. Moira liked her. Coming back from one of their walks her mother
told her a man had called.
"Who was it?" She asked.
"He didn't give his name but said he would call back." Her mother
replied, then saw her reaction. "What's wrong?"
Moira shook her head and reached for her phone to text Mike, fear and
nausea wiping away the peace she had felt since she arrived home. She
sent him a message – *just got a call from a man who wouldn't give his*
name, can you check it out please? She gave him her parents' phone
number and a rough time of when the man had called. Mike got back to
her within the hour. *Not the bad man – we have him under control. Call*
came from California. Enjoy cold Canada. Mike.
But by then she already knew the answer – It was Dan calling to wish
her a Merry Christmas.
It was a short visit, which was how she had planned it – she loved her
parents but knew she would start to feel claustrophobic if she stayed
too long and before the New Year she was on the plane heading back to
Philadelphia.

Dan was in California. For the past seven years he and Holly had spent
Christmas with her parents in cold Michigan and for six of the seven it
had been agony for him as they play-acted a happy couple. So this year
it was back to the warmth of California where he grew up and where his
father still lived with his second wife. But he was restless and at loose

165

ends. Christmas brought into focus that he had to re-establish his life as an individual instead of half of a couple – And the events of the past few months were ever present, still unresolved, acute and disturbing.

It was five months since Ted's uncle had returned Dan's call and had learnt about his nephew's death, and while Dan was in California he hoped to meet him in person.

The uncle had given him his address and now Dan started out, travelling south towards Paso Robles. He took the scenic route down the Pacific Coast Highway.... *right along the edge of the world he had thought as a child....* He took his time, savoring the magnificent scenery. *This is what I've missed he thought* ... It brought back many memories.

At Cambria he turned inland and took highway 46 towards Paso Robles. In the last twenty years the area had changed completely from deep avocado country to a new wine mecca. On his way he passed winery after winery, and when he finally reached the address, he realized that Ted's uncle was part of the new culture. He found him in the wine tasting room.

They talked for hours. He and Ted's mother had grown up in California, and he had lived there all his life only moving from Sonoma to Paso Robles several years ago – "When Sonoma got too crowded."

He told Dan about the break-up of Ted's parents while they were in England, and how his father had stayed there and pretty much disappeared after a terrible divorce.

"And my sister never got over it, she stayed bitter for the rest of her life, wouldn't let his father have any contact with Ted – threw away the letters he wrote him. Poor little boy, I felt so sorry for him. It changed him. And it looked like he'd just found a girl and was finally happy when he was killed. What a waste!"

They were getting morose. Dan decided he'd tasted more than enough wine and said his goodbyes, inviting the uncle to call him if he ever got to New York.

He drove north on the quickest route back to his father's home. He had a lot to think about. He hoped Holly wasn't going to turn into a permanently bitter person like Ted's mother. He decided he would call her to see how her Christmas was going, they needed to talk –civilly, without emotion – and maybe finally they would be able to put a true

166

end to their marriage and both move on with their lives. He didn't want her to stay miserable for the rest of her life.

As soon as he arrived home he acted on his decision and managed to reach Holly in Michigan. They talked for a while – *It was a start, he thought...*

Later he tried to call Moira, but she was out. He told her mother he would call back.

Meanwhile Mike was chasing bad guys on the other side of the world, Christmas Day passed without him realizing it......

TWENTY-FOUR

The New Year came in with the usual intense, phony celebrations. For Joan and Tom, the New Year only emphasized the void Jill's death had left. It was raw and unresolved. They were managing to lean on each other but they grieved in different ways and were not always in step. They were thankful for their marriage which was long-standing and solid and for most of the time they managed to give each other the support they needed. It would take time, but they would find a way to get through it, changed – but they would survive.

Dan was beginning to realize he had to resolve his angry feelings for Holly before he could move on with his life. Talking with Ted's uncle had made him realize how bitter Holly must be about their breakup – he did not want her to become like Ted's mother, wounded for life. He had to make her understand how bad they were for each other and try to diffuse the horrible negative feelings they both harbored.

Moira was still feeling anxious and insecure – totally new sensations for her before the events of last summer. She had always been outgoing and confident. Making decisions had always come easily to her. Very rarely did she have second thoughts, she naturally assumed her choices were correct – it had given her the freedom to enjoy life. And she had enjoyed meeting new people. But now she was suspicious of every stranger she saw looking in her direction, untrusting of everyone – including herself. She questioned her own judgement constantly. She was having a hard time concentrating on her work... *Should I get a new*

job?.... Should I move?... Get away from here?... Would it help?...
Where would I go?... Would it change anything?... Every now and then
she toyed with a new idea. But a new job away from Philadelphia would
mean she would lose the comfort of being able to reach out to Mike
every time she had a suspicion, and that would make her feel even less
safe. She thought about New York, she knew she would be able to
advance her career there, but that would mean she had moved closer to
Dan, so she nixed that idea too. She had to get her confidence back
without Dan or anyone else's help. This was something she had to do by
herself. Besides she felt she had burnt her bridges with Dan and it
wasn't clear in her head how much she cared about that. She decided
to stay put. In her saner moments she had to admit that no one had
followed her recently.

And with all of this the puppet master Mike held their future security in
his hands as he and his team worked at taking down the network that
had caused the deaths of Ted and Jill. Every now and then he would
update them with the news of another arrest, tell them that they were
another step closer to eliminating the far-flung organization, and nearer
to solving the puzzle of why it had been created.
True to his personality he kept most what he knew close to his chest,
only sharing the odd piece of information when he absolutely had to.
His record of getting results was recognized within the Company and
consequently he had a freer hand than most to carry out his
investigations. But he still pushed the limits, giving only a passing nod to
authority and often taking his own council over that of the Company's
when the two clashed. And now he was pushing hard .... He knew that
he was tracking down a brand new organization with branches in eight
countries. But their motive still puzzled him. Their actions did not hang
together to make a cohesive whole. What was their aim? The facts he
had discovered so far were still much too diffuse for his liking. As usual
he had to figure out the patterns and interactions of all branches of the
organization – proving or discarding every thesis, it took time. Only after
that, when he had finally interlocked the pieces with absolute certainty,
would he go public. He was driving himself and his is team hard.

But no one had forgotten Ted and Jill, or their senseless deaths. They were missed every day.

By the end of February everyone was fed up to the teeth with the never ending blizzards and ice, praying for an early end to the ghastly winter. The snowfalls and the frigid weather of the last few months had broken all records.

Moira was in New York for a meeting which finished by late morning and she found herself alone and at loose ends. She had thought about Dan often since Christmas when he had called. It had lifted her spirits more than she had wanted to admit. Now she realized she was within walking distance of his office and on a whim decided to see if he was free. She asked the uniformed man at the front desk to find out if he was available, adding she did not have an appointment.

Pretty soon a woman came out of one of the elevators and came up to her, inviting her to follow, Mr. Murphy was available. The elevator took them to the fifth floor and the woman escorted her to Dan's office before returning to her desk in front of the elevators.

Dan rose from his desk and came across the room, pushing the door closed behind her. Suddenly Moira was very glad she had come and hoped that closing the door meant he would kiss her – but he didn't. "God, it's good to see you," he said. "I've missed you."

He was being very careful, not knowing why she had shown up so unexpectedly – not wanting to scare her away. He sensed that she was feeling as awkward as he was and resisted the urge to ask her why she had come. After a few minutes of casual conversation, he made a move. "Let's get out of here. Got time for lunch?"

They had a long lunch. Their last real conversation had been at Jill's Memorial, and a lot had happened since then. It took time to fill in all the petty details of their lives since that last face to face back in October. And they were both being very cautious, neither knew how solid their footing was, neither wanted to screw things up now they were back talking again. Gradually their polite, trivial day-to-day conversation moved on to subjects with more substance, becoming more personal. Dan told her about meeting with Ted's uncle in California and related how the uncle had told him about Ted's parents divorcing and how bitter Ted's mother was for the rest of her life.

170

"It made me look at Holly differently," he said. "I don't want her to waste her life like Ted's mother did. I called her up and we are trying to lose some of the anger and bitterness we both have so we can move forward with our separate lives."
Moira was glad.
"Is it working?" She asked.
"It will take time, but we're making progress." He said.
He changed the subject and asked if she was still seeing Mike.
"That finished before Thanksgiving." She said.
"I'm so sorry." Dan said, feigning sympathy.
"Don't be," she replied. "It was totally mutual, we both just looked at each other one day and realized we had run out the string. I told you it wasn't a long term thing. And we are still friends, which is great."
Moira checked the time – they had been talking for over three hours.
"I'm going to have to hustle to catch my train." She said.
"Why don't you miss it?" He asked, only half in jest.
"No I have to get back." She answered.
They caught a cab to Penn Station and he came into the station with her. This time he did kiss her. Then looked into her face and smiled broadly.
"I'll pick you up at your apartment Friday evening at seven." He said.
"No ifs or buts, I'm coming, we're going out to dinner."
"I'd like that." Moira answered, and gave him her address.

Friday evening promptly at seven, her doorbell rang. She opened the door and he came in, put his arms around her and they kissed, both glad that they had finally managed to get together again.
"You ready?" He said. "We'd better get out of here or we'll never make it to the restaurant."
As Moira guessed Dan had picked a quiet place where they could talk and unlike their last – and only dinner together they drank conservatively. They wanted to get to know each other on a deeper footing.
Dinner was not a lingering affair and when Moira suggested they could skip the coffee and have it back at her apartment Dan readily agreed. But once back there the coffee was forgotten. They undressed each

other carefully and slowly, enjoying every second. This time they were going to take time exploring their bodies. This time they intended to remember every second of their love making.

TWENTY-FIVE

Throughout the winter and spring months the attempts to bomb corporations had continued. The incidents seemed pretty random except that they were always in the Northeast and every time, luckily, they had been foiled. But every time Dan and Moira and Joan and Tom had wondered if it was the work of the same organization that had killed Ted and Jill. It kept them on edge, they longed for some concrete news, but updates from the FBI were getting further and further apart and they were beginning to fear that they would never get any answers, never find out who had killed Ted and Jill, and why.

Then one day in April, Joan saw on the evening news a video of two men and a woman in handcuffs being escorted off a plane. The newscaster's voice in the background announcing they had been extradited from England to answer terroristic charges and two counts of murder. Joan called Tom and they watched the end of the news item together, both excitedly wondering if this could finally be the answers they had been waiting for, that their daughter's murder had been solved.

The following afternoon Mike called to tell them that they had caught those responsible for Jill's death, and it would not be long before they would have the whole of the network in custody. He promised he would be contacting them again soon. Tom and Joan were elated. Finally, there was light at the end of the tunnel!

Joan was up early the next morning, and for the first time in many months felt almost happiness. She was anxious to let Moira know the good news and called her right after breakfast.

Moira was thrilled. It was Saturday morning and she shook Dan awake and told him why Joan had called.

"Finally! Thank God!" He said and pulled her to him. Then he added, suddenly serious. "Do you realize we would never have met if it hadn't been for Ted and Jill?"

She propped herself up on her elbow and looked at him.

"I hate to think of their deaths being the reason we're together, I think about them all the time. I fantasize that we would finally have met anyway. Ted was your friend, and Jill was mine. Maybe they would have set up a blind date for us, or maybe they would have given a party and we would have met there…"

"You're a true romantic" He teased, stroking the profile of her body. He grinned. "Do you remember telling me you didn't want to channel their lives, one weekend here, one weekend in New York?"

"Well that was then and this is now – and a lot of couples do what we are doing, not just Ted and Jill."

"And," he said, "Do you remember when I teased you that we should duplicate their trip to England you said, no you'd rather go to Italy?"

She rolled over on her back and giggled, "Let's do both." She said.

"That's a plan." He said and leant over and kissed her.

The attempts to bomb corporations became less frequent and then stopped completely. None had succeeded. In May Mike called Dan to let him know that all those involved in the bombing attempts had been caught and that yes, they were part of the same network that was being rounded up. Dan thanked him for the information and once again Mike thanked Dan for wearing a wire and being an integral part of catching the first bomber. Neither man mentioned Moira…

Memorial Day came and went, followed by June with no further news. And then it was July. Independence Day was a beautiful day in the Northeast. Another milestone passed. It was now almost exactly a year since ted had been killed.

TWENTY-SIX

Mike was sitting at his desk – a rarity for him – mentally checking off that everything was done. It always gave him a great feeling of satisfaction when he had finally solved the puzzle and put everything to rights. Finally the last few tentacles of the network were eliminated. He had interviewed all of the people they had in custody and had given a detailed presentation of his findings to the powers that be.

He pushed away from his desk and rocked his chair back on two legs. The wrap up was complete.... *Time to call Moira* – He had purposely left that for last. It would not be complete for him until Moira knew everything. She had been there from the beginning and had made an impression on him right from that first meeting in the FBI Building. Her intensity and determination to get to the bottom of why her friend had been killed had stuck with him. He grinned as he thought about her – remembering how she got under his skin and the good times they had had together ... and the number of times she had made him furious. It would be good to see her again.

They agreed to meet for a drink in a hotel bar close to her office.

As usual he was there first, as usual busy on his phone. He saw her come in the door and as usual watched as she came towards him. Something was different – the aura of sexuality she radiated had changed, somehow was more controlled, less accessible. *She's not available any more he thought.* He wondered who she was involved with and wondered if she realized how much she had changed ... She came up to him smiling and gave him a friendly kiss before she sat down.

"You're glowing!" He joked. "Who is it?"

"Dan." She said simply.

He was genuinely happy for her.

"Did I ever tell you how he balled me out at the Memorial for Jill? Told me not to hurt you, not to toy with your feelings."

"No! What did you say to him?"

"I told him you were a big girl and could look after yourself – that really made him mad - I think he would have punched me out if we'd been anywhere else... obviously it didn't stop us being together – and he didn't get me to back off.... Just the opposite." He added with a grin.

A light bulb lit up... *That's why Dan changed after that day...*

He got down to the reason they were sitting there – the wrap up – she was anxious to learn everything, she needed to know the cause of all the turmoil and pain of the past year. What it was it all about – what was this organization – what were they trying to do –why had Ted and Jill been killed?

It turned out to be a fairly simple explanation –simple, far reaching, evil. Mike began: "Picture an octopus – eight tentacles, eight different countries, right? A group of mostly ex-military, over the hill men of different nationalities, all with grudges against either the military and, or the establishment in their country, decided to form a secret organization and hire out to whoever would pay for their services. No principles, just in it for the money and the jollies. They looked at the unrest in the world today, saw an opportunity and seized on it."

He paused, searching for the correct words to express his feelings. "Psychopaths all of them. Totally disassociated from society. It was like one giant video game to them..." Then he added disgustedly.... "But after all, this was a secret society, so if a few good people got killed along the way when they threatened their secret, it was justified, right?"

He went on with his explanation. "Last summer they were at the very beginning of setting up the organization. Each chapter was set up the same way at the same time – that's why it took so long to run down all the members, they were scattered in different countries and there was no history behind them. Each chapter had to prove itself. The goal of the branch here in the Northeast was to cause mayhem by bombing

corporations, they weren't very good at it thank God. The Devon branch was more organized. Their goal was to take over a military camp in a remote part of Devon to prove their worth. Ted just happened to get in the way – he could identify them so they pushed him over the cliff."
 "Why Jill?"
"She wouldn't accept Ted's death and was digging into what had really happened, she wouldn't let it go, so they killed her too."
"But why the toothpicks? Moira asked "That seemed so totally bizarre but that was the start of everything for Ted and Jill."
"None of the potential members knew each other – obviously every chapter needed to get together to form their nucleus. They were afraid of the internet or any form of social media, because it might be monitored, so they resorted to a very basic method, nobody would think of tracking toothpicks. Everyone who got a toothpick was tagged to be part of the leadership of that branch. Each was given only enough information to find their own toothpick."
Another long pause, Mike watching Moira's reaction, waiting for her questions, giving her time to take everything in .... *And to prolong their time together... He was going to miss her...* He continued.
"Ted was not the only person who answered the ads. Similar ads were placed in newspapers in the other countries as well, but the other people just planted their toothpicks and went on their way, they weren't curious like Ted. And he was correct about the significance of his toothpicks' locations– they triangulated on the military compound on the Burrows in North Devon."
"Poor Ted." She said.
He was silent for a moment then said quietly, almost to himself,
"It's always the ramifications that leave the bad taste."
He shook off his moment of introspection and paused for a moment more before he stood up and looked down at Moira.
"I'm off! My new adventure beckons. Take care of yourself."
He stroked her hair.
"Have a good life."
"You too." She said.

But he was already out the door.

ABOUT THE AUTHOR

Maggie grew up in England on the North Devon Coast.
After college she decided to take five years and work her way around the
world. She started out in Canada, but on her second stop, in Washington
D.C., she met her husband and the world trip was changed to exploring life
in the United States. She and the family have lived and worked all over the
Country from California to Connecticut with many stops in-between.
She now lives in Upstate New York.

Made in the USA
Charleston, SC
21 November 2016